BEAUTY
AND THE
SQUAT
BEARS

ÉMILE
BRAVO

J-GN
BEAUTY AND THE
        SQUAT BEARS
399-8633

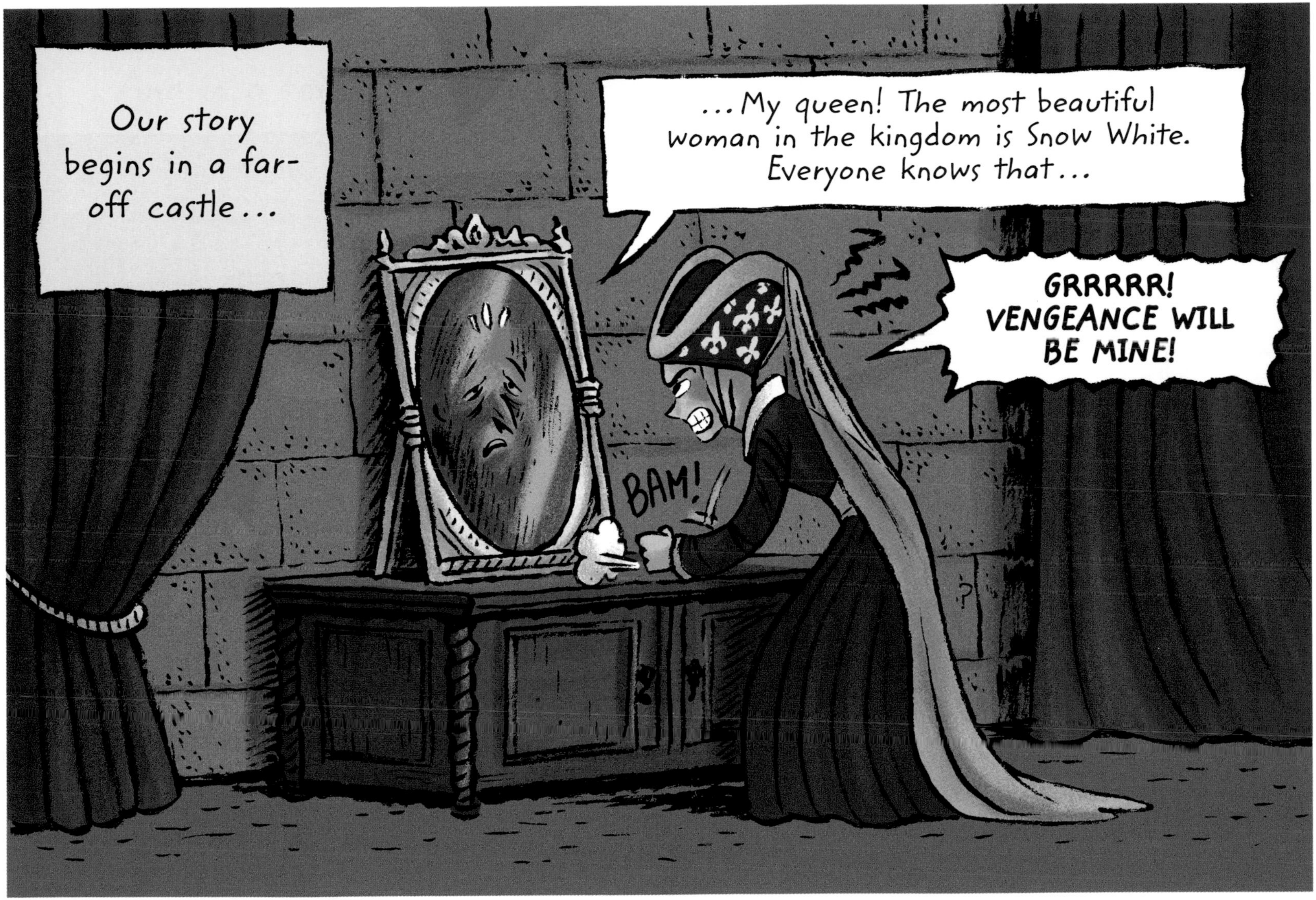
Our story begins in a far-off castle...
...My queen! The most beautiful woman in the kingdom is Snow White. Everyone knows that...
GRRRRR! VENGEANCE WILL BE MINE!
BAM!

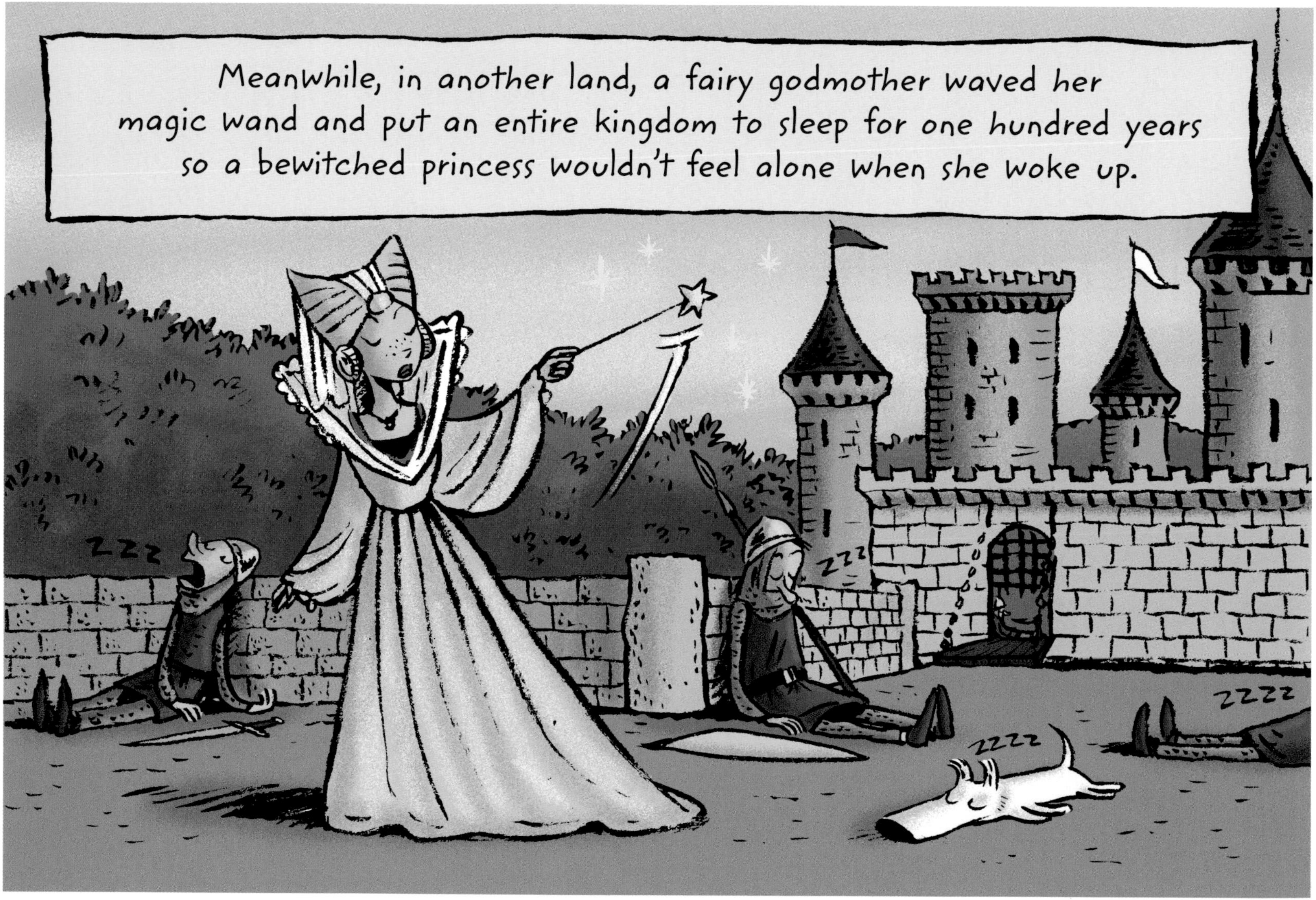
Meanwhile, in another land, a fairy godmother waved her magic wand and put an entire kingdom to sleep for one hundred years so a bewitched princess wouldn't feel alone when she woke up.
ZZZ
ZZZ
ZZZZ
ZZZZ

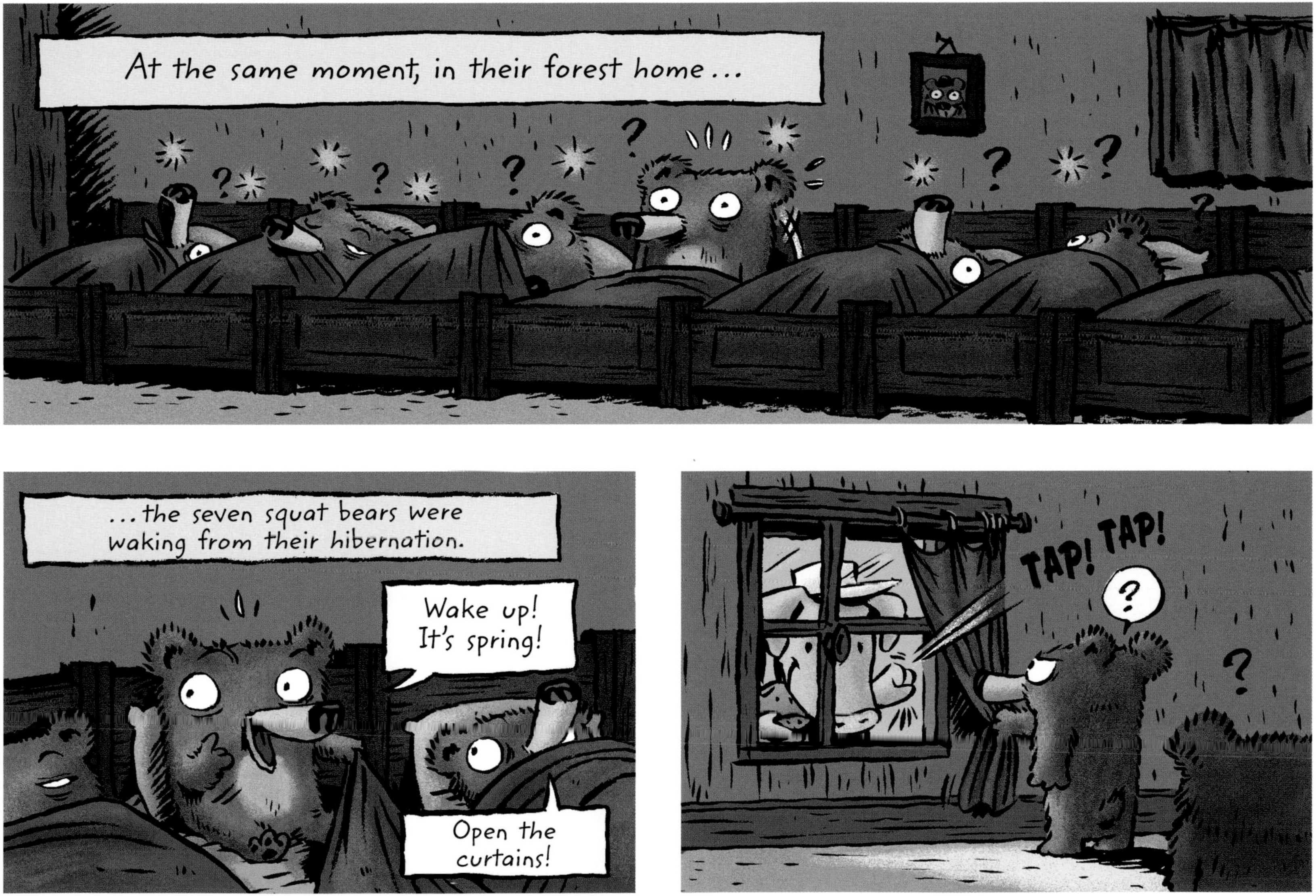
At the same moment, in their forest home...
...the seven squat bears were waking from their hibernation.
Wake up! It's spring!
Open the curtains!
TAP! TAP!

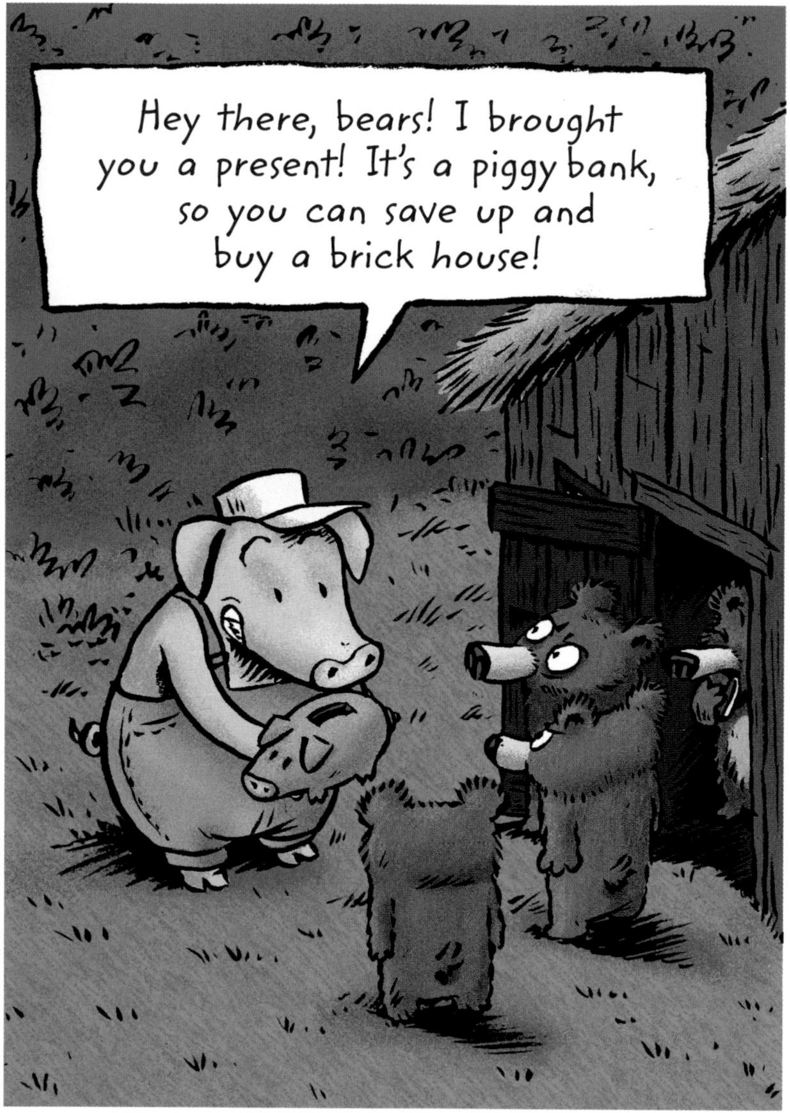
Hey there, bears! I brought you a present! It's a piggy bank, so you can save up and buy a brick house!

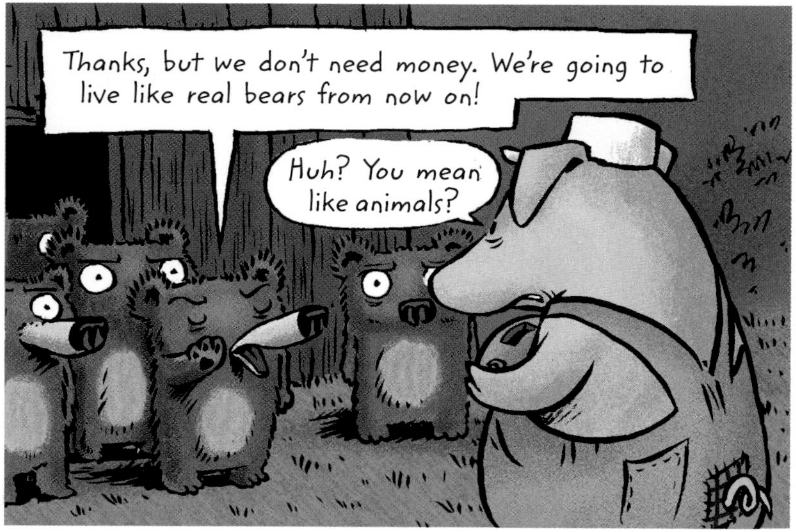
Thanks, but we don't need money. We're going to live like real bears from now on!
Huh? You mean like animals?

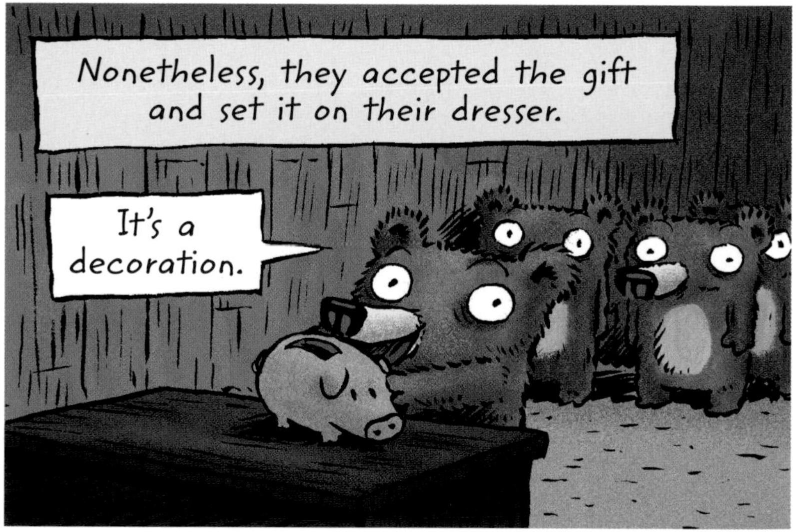
Nonetheless, they accepted the gift and set it on their dresser.
It's a decoration.

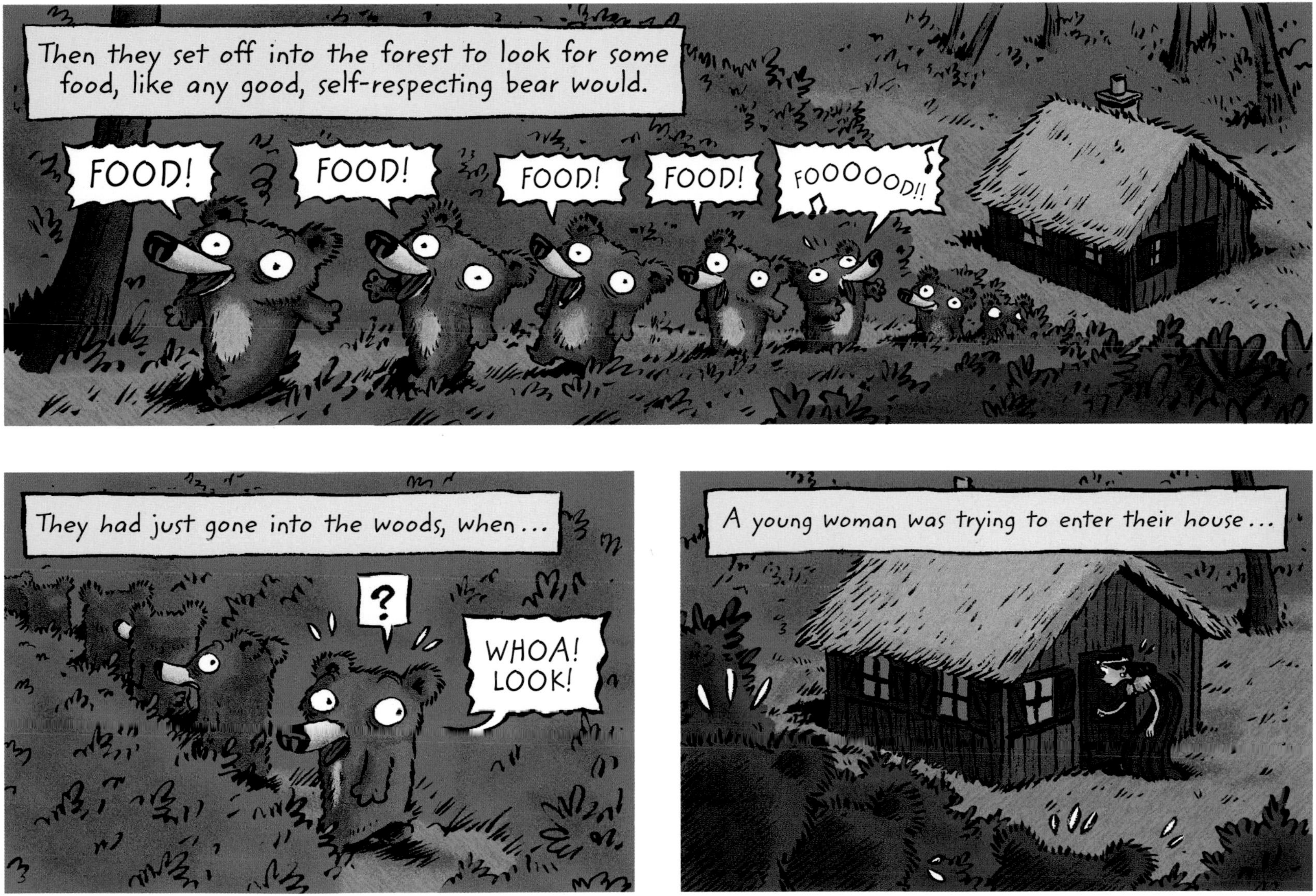
Then they set off into the forest to look for some food, like any good, self-respecting bear would.
FOOD!
FOOD!
FOOD!
FOOD!
FOOOOOOD!!
They had just gone into the woods, when...
?
WHOA! LOOK!
A young woman was trying to enter their house...

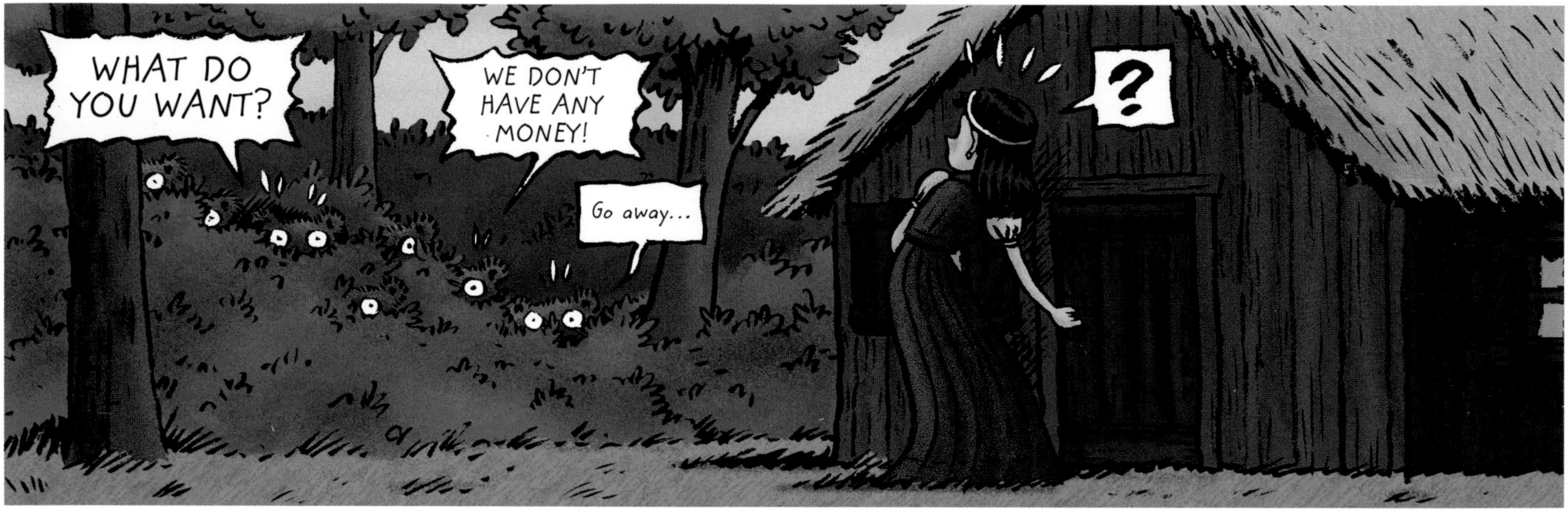
WHAT DO YOU WANT?
WE DON'T HAVE ANY MONEY!
Go away...
?

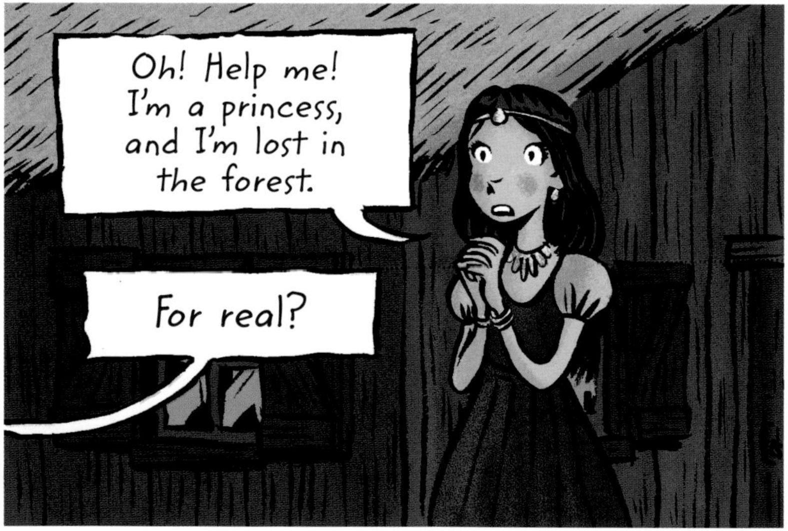
Oh! Help me! I'm a princess, and I'm lost in the forest.
For real?

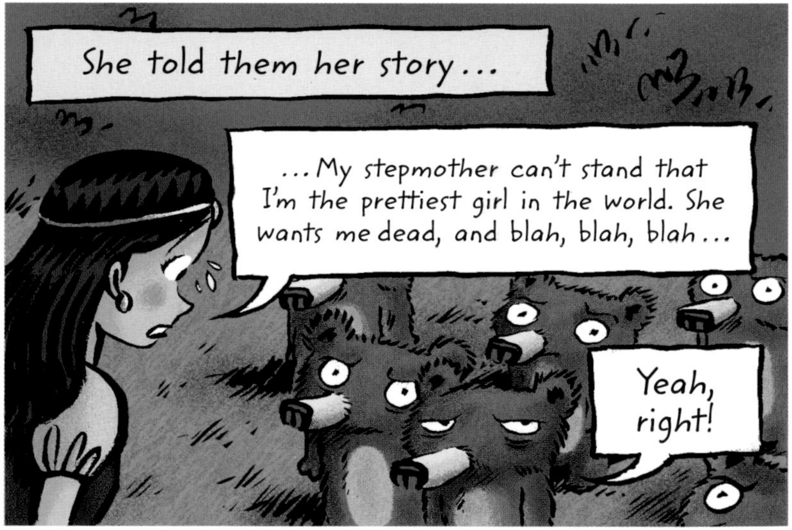
She told them her story...
...My stepmother can't stand that I'm the prettiest girl in the world. She wants me dead, and blah, blah, blah...
Yeah, right!

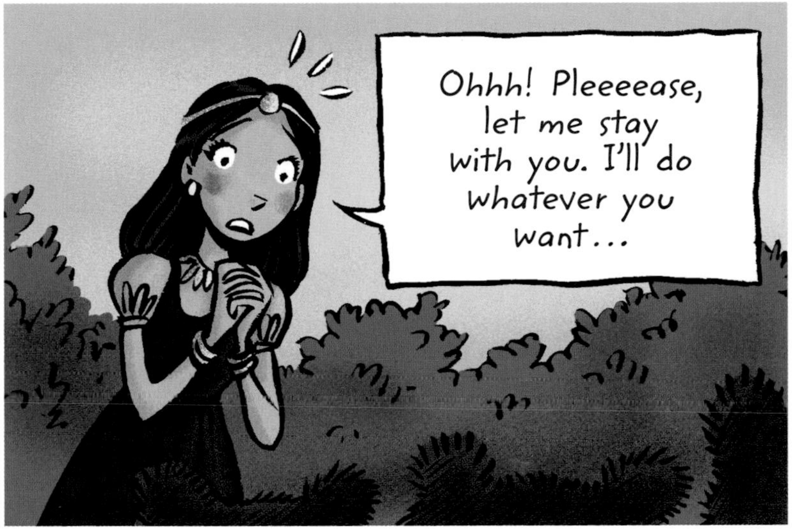
Ohhh! Pleeeease, let me stay with you. I'll do whatever you want...

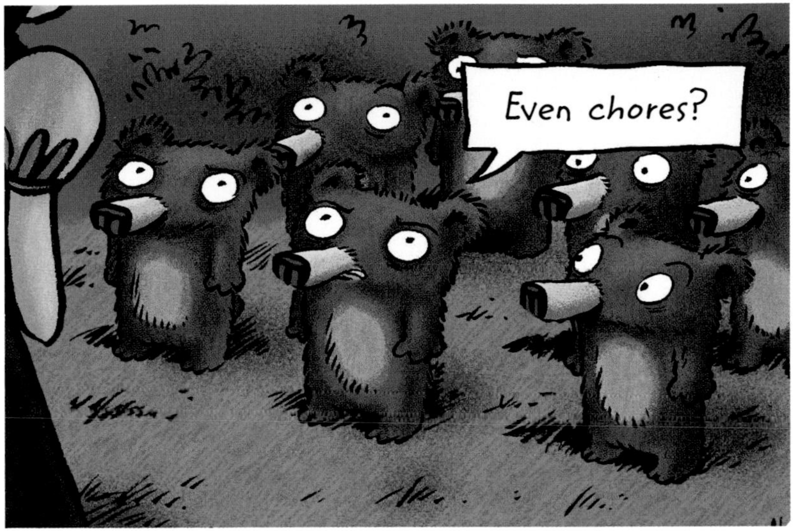
Even chores?

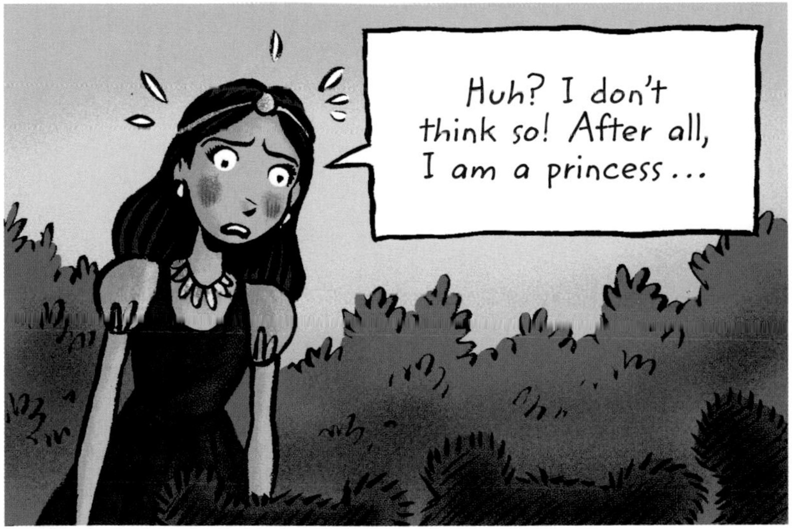
Huh? I don't think so! After all, I am a princess...

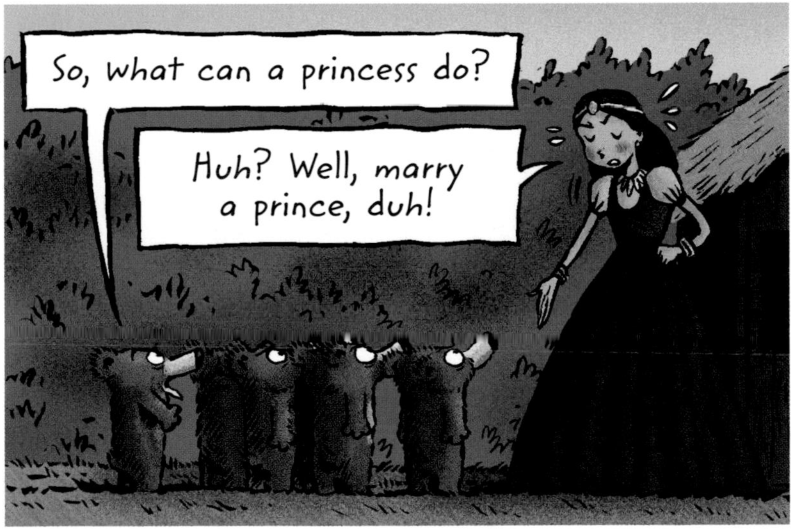
So, what can a princess do?
Huh? Well, marry a prince, duh!

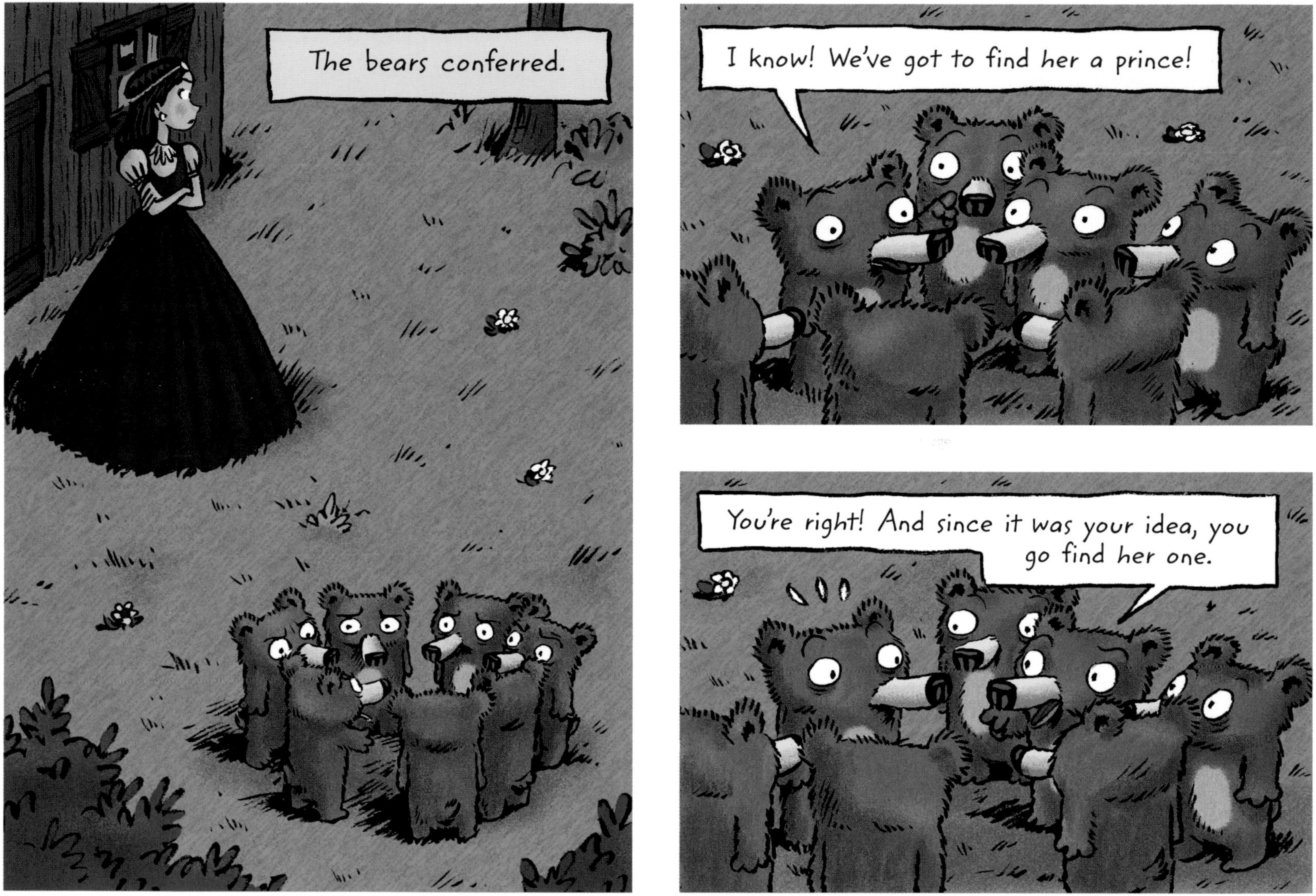
The bears conferred.
I know! We've got to find her a prince!
You're right! And since it was your idea, you go find her one.

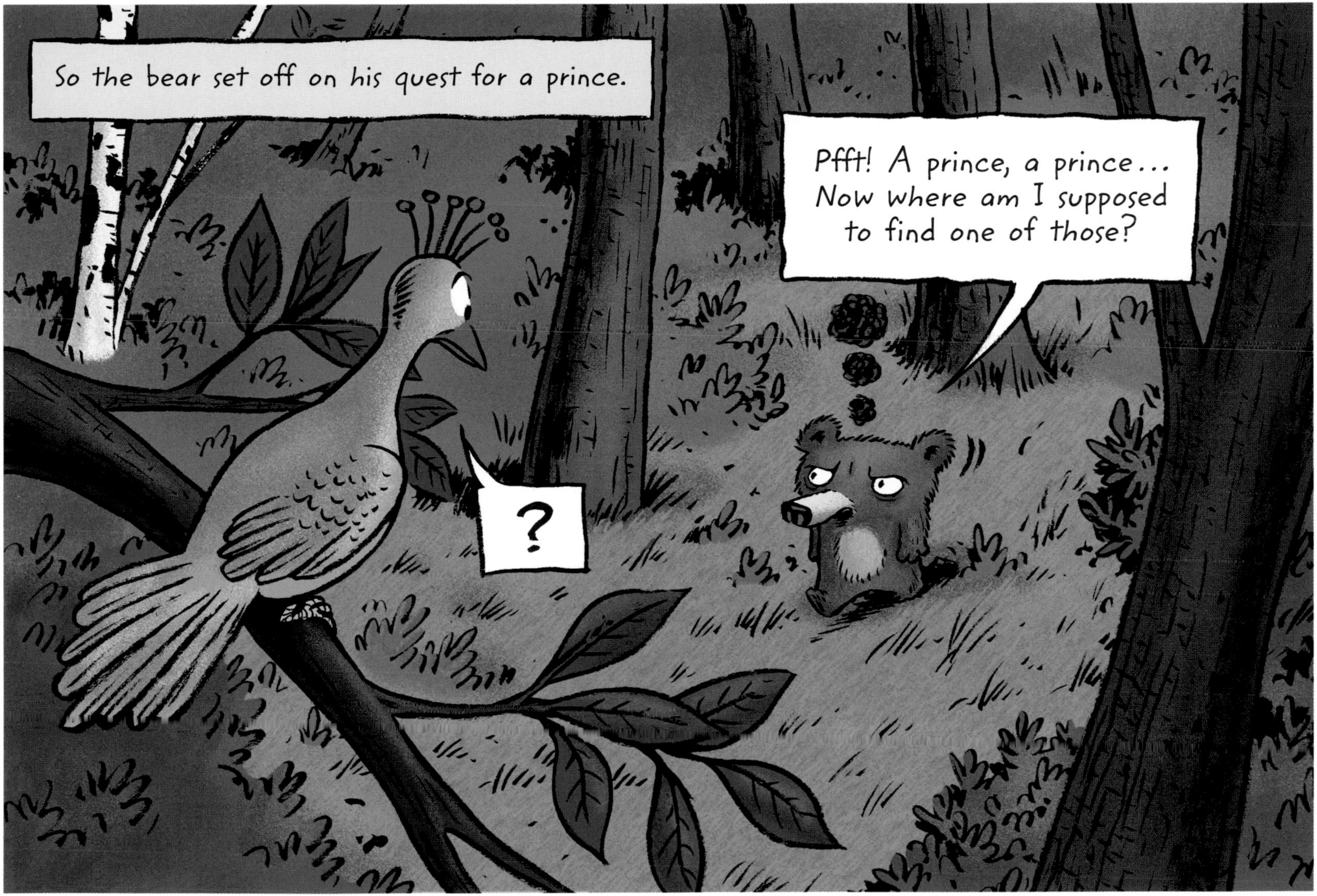
So the bear set off on his quest for a prince.
?
Pfft! A prince, a prince... Now where am I supposed to find one of those?

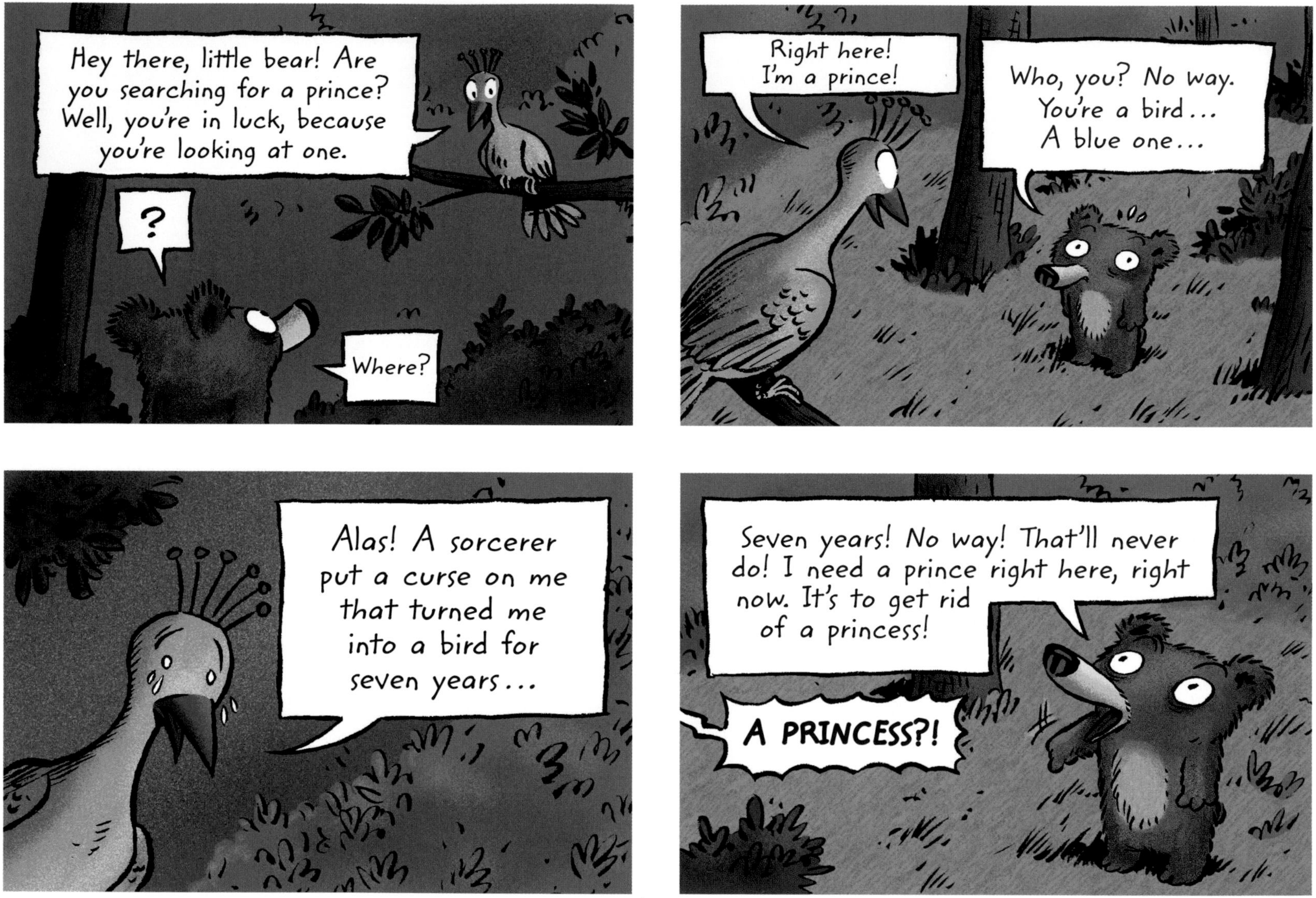
Hey there, little bear! Are you searching for a prince? Well, you're in luck, because you're looking at one.
?
Where?
Right here! I'm a prince!
Who, you? No way. You're a bird... A blue one...
Alas! A sorcerer put a curse on me that turned me into a bird for seven years...
Seven years! No way! That'll never do! I need a prince right here, right now. It's to get rid of a princess!
A PRINCESS?!

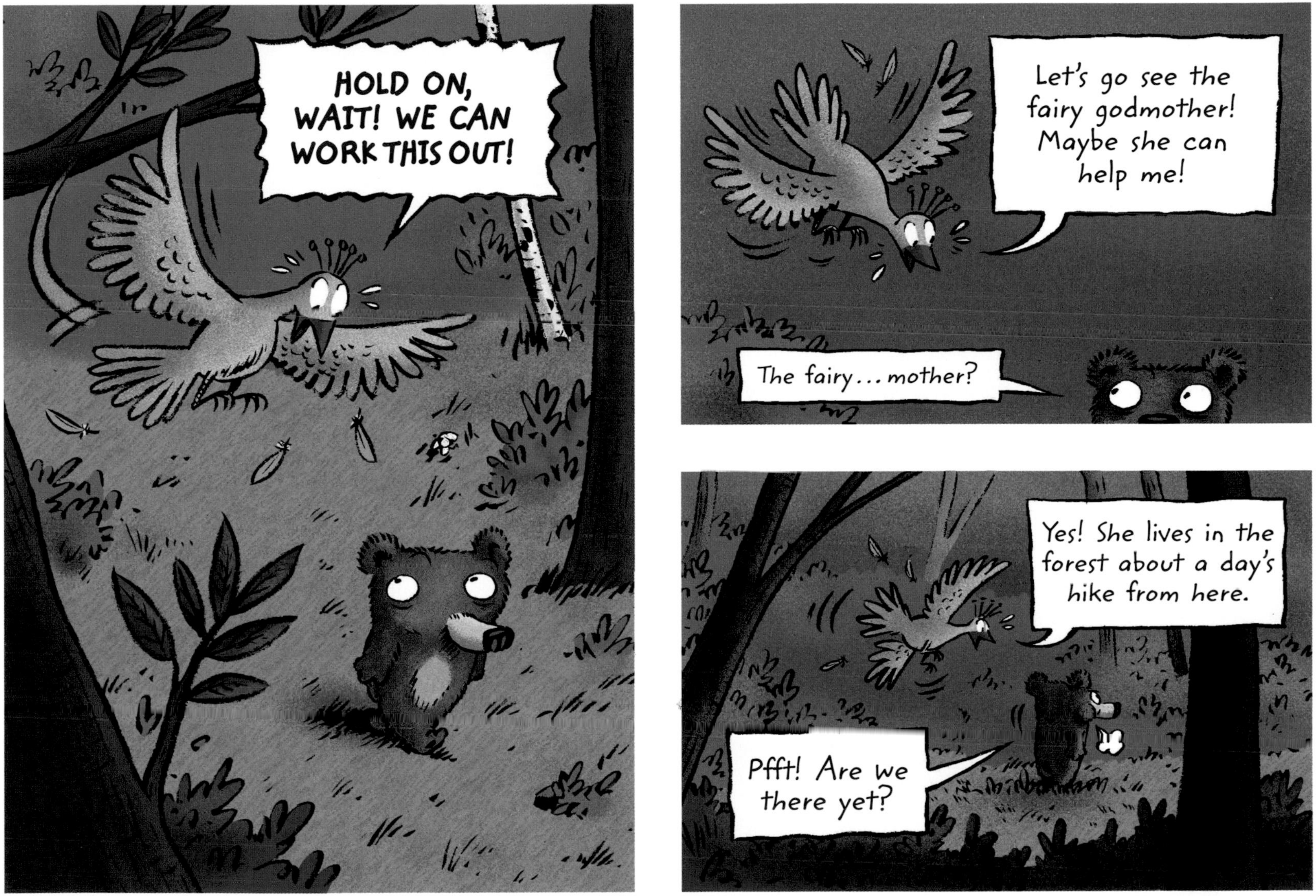

HOLD ON, WAIT! WE CAN WORK THIS OUT!
Let's go see the fairy godmother! Maybe she can help me!
The fairy... mother?
Yes! She lives in the forest about a day's hike from here.
Pfft! Are we there yet?

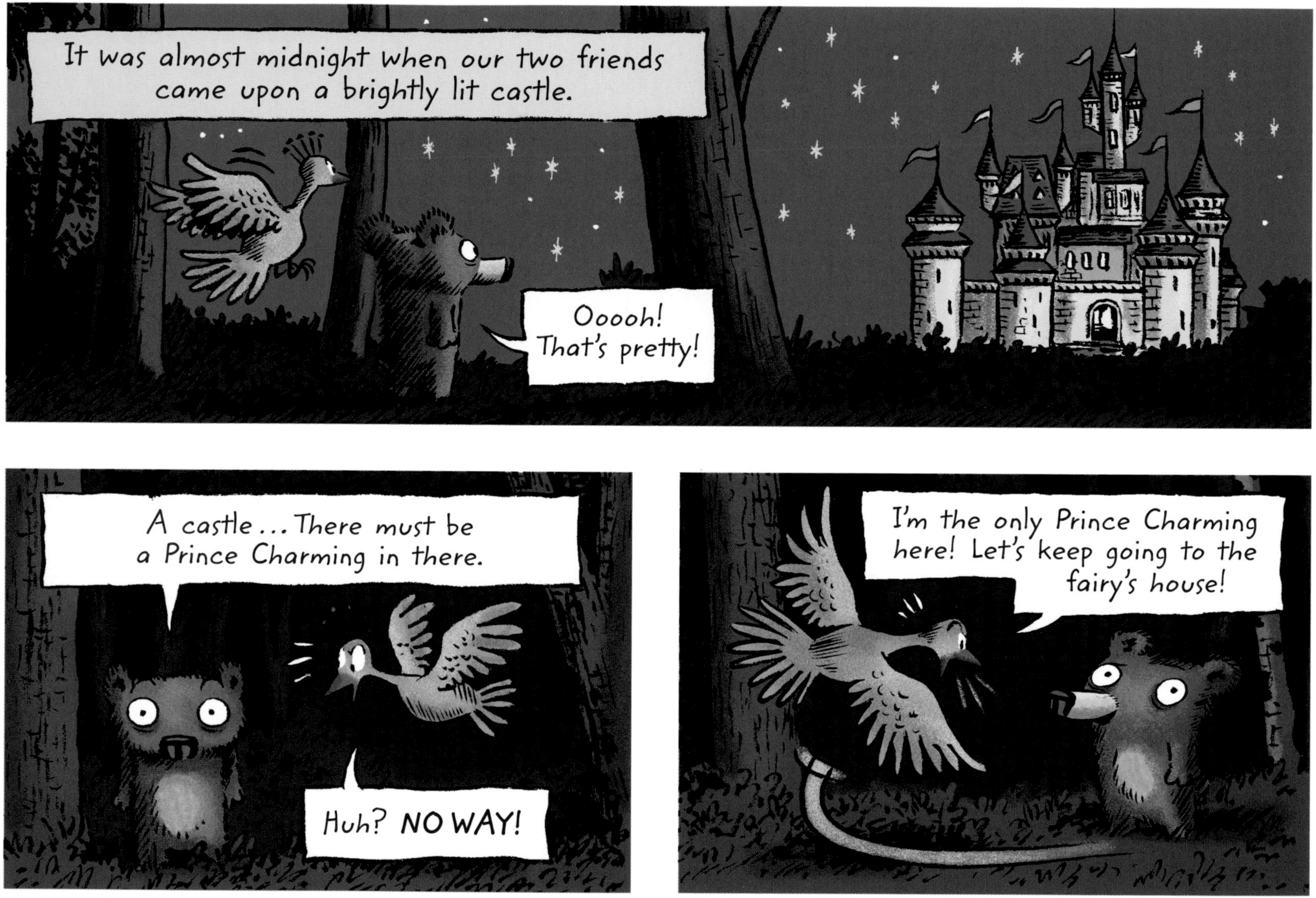
It was almost midnight when our two friends came upon a brightly lit castle.
Ooooh! That's pretty!
A castle... There must be a Prince Charming in there.
Huh? NO WAY!
I'm the only Prince Charming here! Let's keep going to the fairy's house!

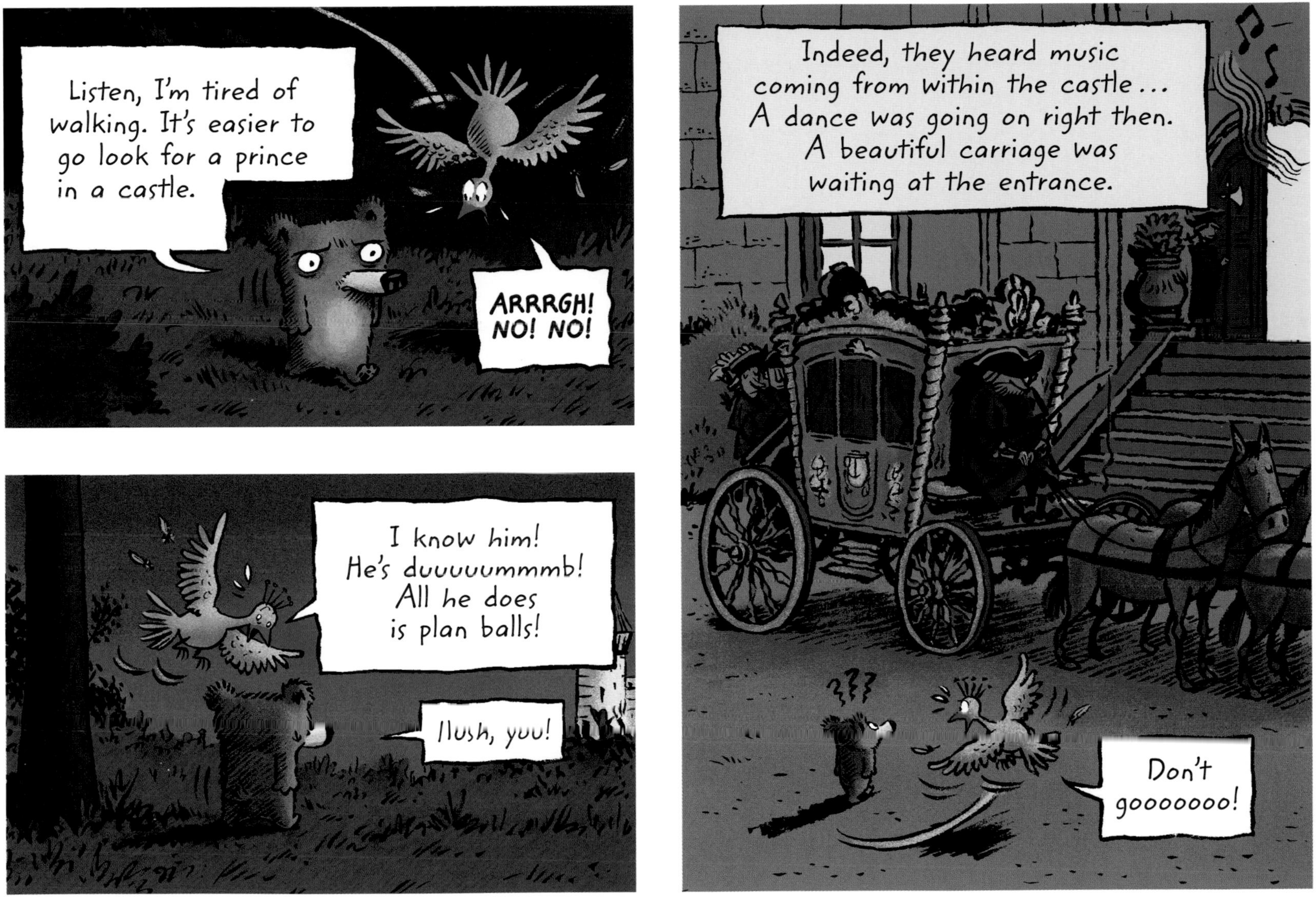
Listen, I'm tired of walking. It's easier to go look for a prince in a castle.
ARRRGH! NO! NO!
I know him! He's duuuuummmb! All he does is plan balls!
Hush, you!
Indeed, they heard music coming from within the castle... A dance was going on right then. A beautiful carriage was waiting at the entrance.
Don't gooooooo!

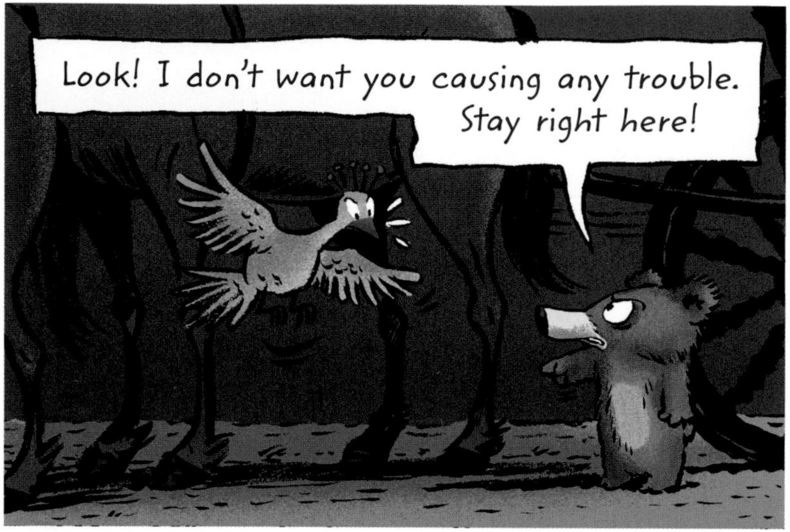
Look! I don't want you causing any trouble. Stay right here!

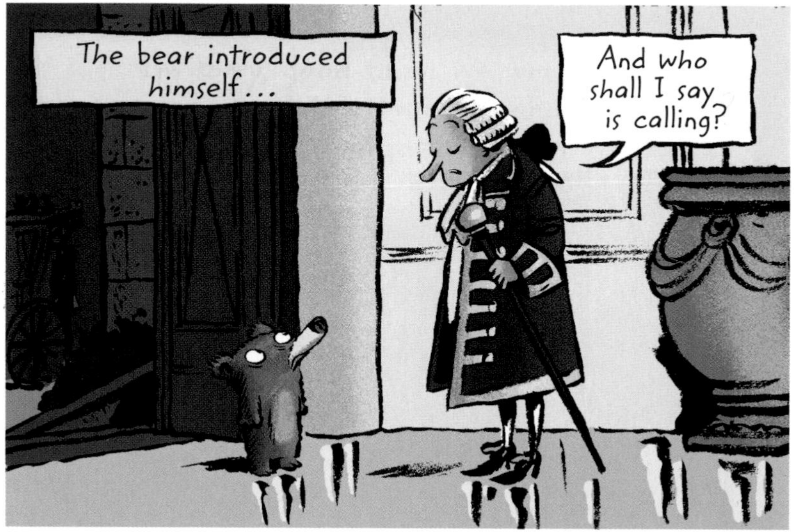
The bear introduced himself...
And who shall I say is calling?

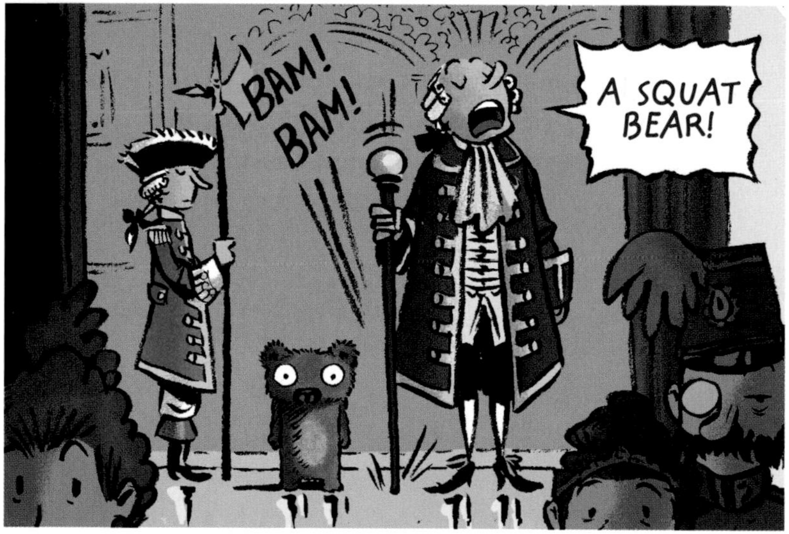
BAM! BAM!
A SQUAT BEAR!

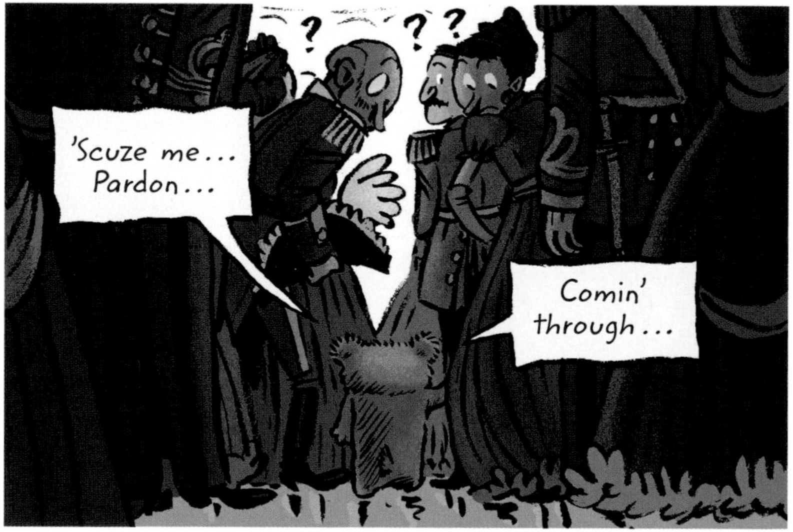
'Scuze me... Pardon...
Comin' through...

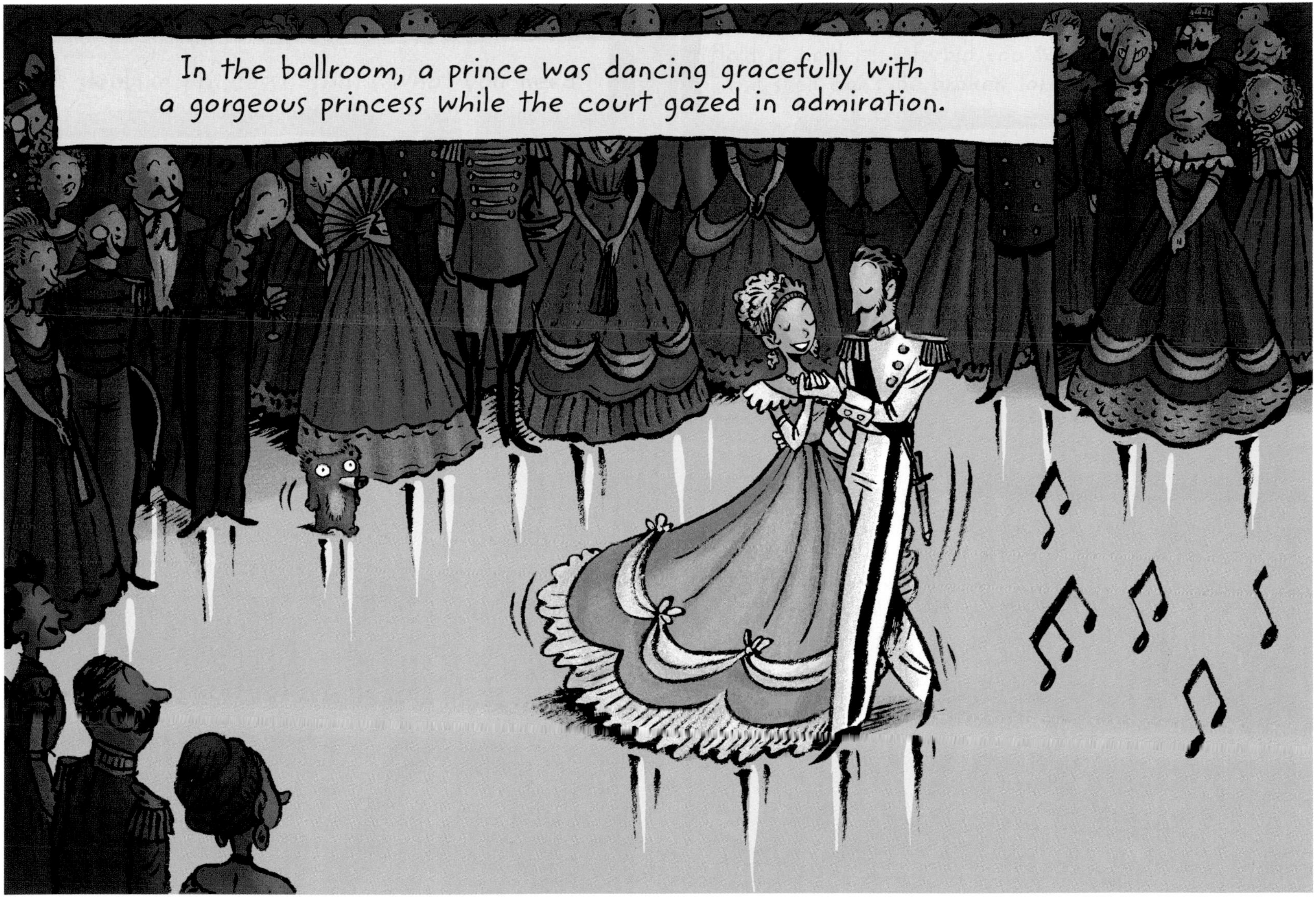
In the ballroom, a prince was dancing gracefully with a gorgeous princess while the court gazed in admiration.

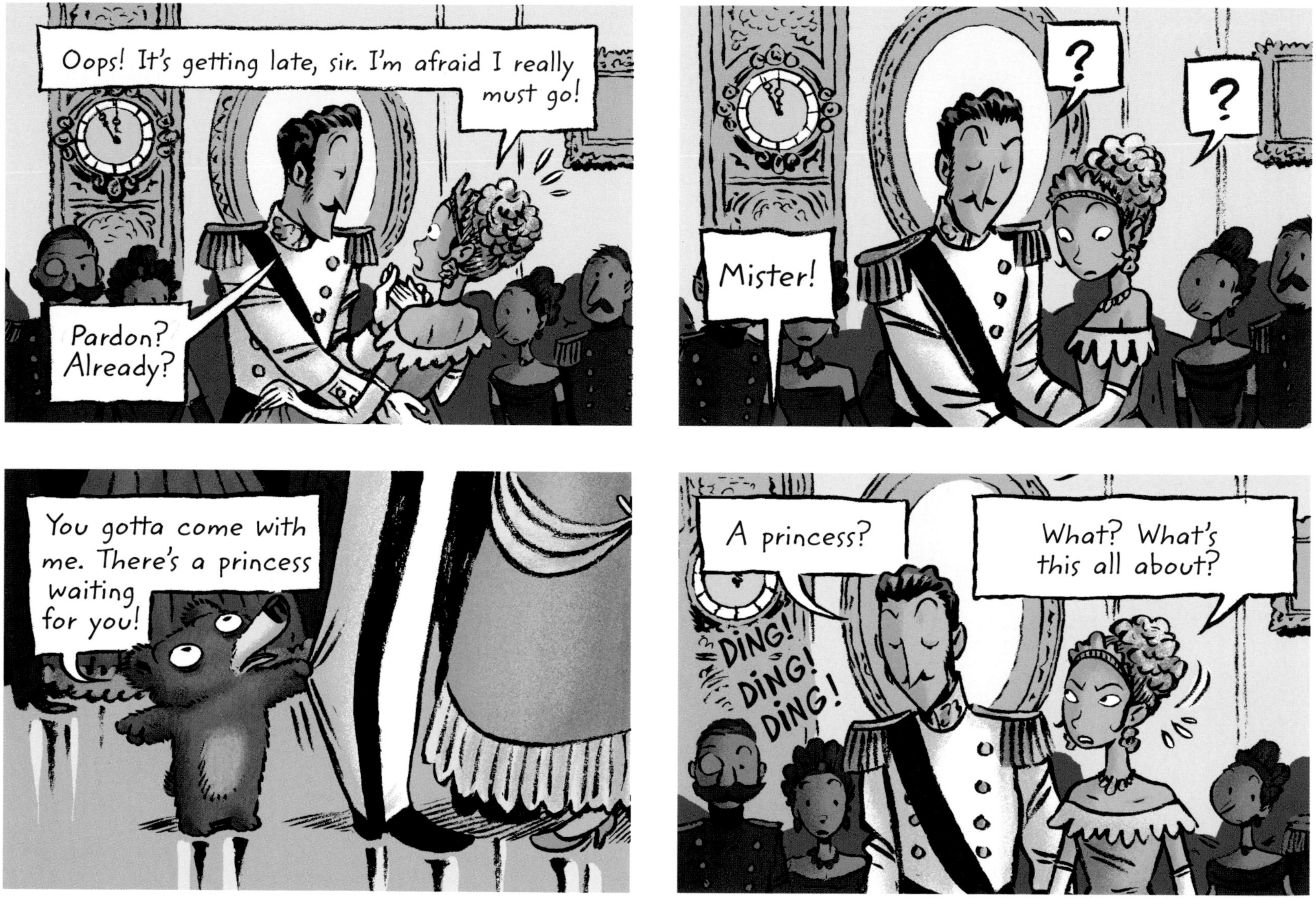
Oops! It's getting late, sir. I'm afraid I really must go!
Pardon? Already?
?
?
Mister!
You gotta come with me. There's a princess waiting for you!
A princess?
What? What's this all about?
DING! DING! DING!

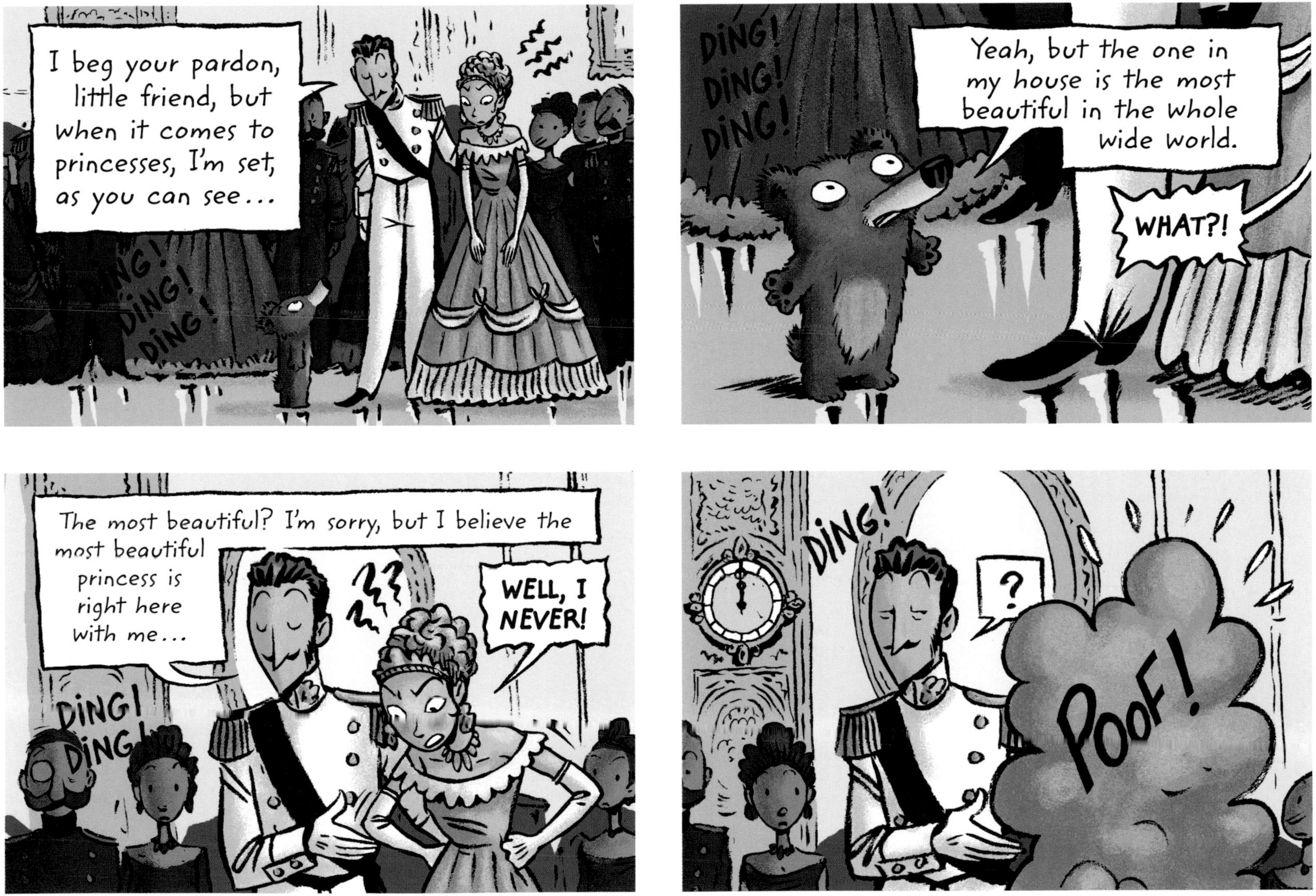
I beg your pardon, little friend, but when it comes to princesses, I'm set, as you can see...
DING! DING! DING!
DING! DING! DING!
Yeah, but the one in my house is the most beautiful in the whole wide world.
WHAT?!
The most beautiful? I'm sorry, but I believe the most beautiful princess is right here with me...
WELL, I NEVER!
DING! DING!
DING!
?
POOF!

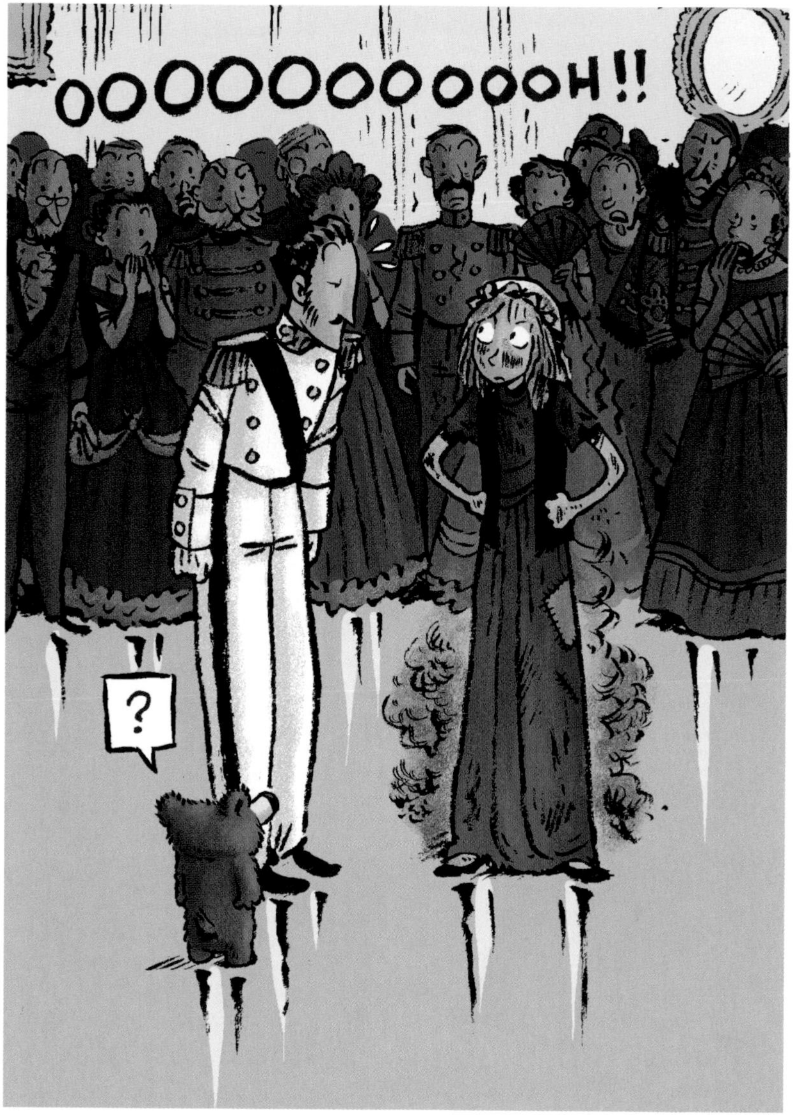
OOOOOOOOOOOH!!
?

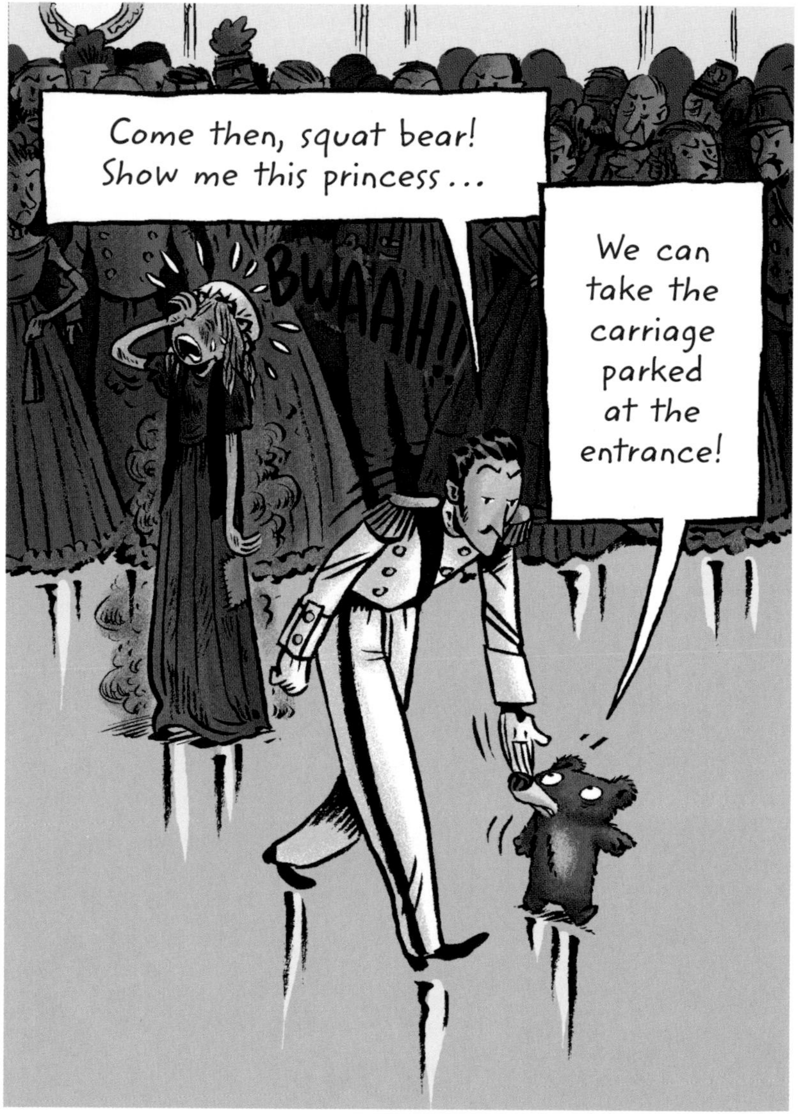
Come then, squat bear! Show me this princess...
BWAAH!!
We can take the carriage parked at the entrance!

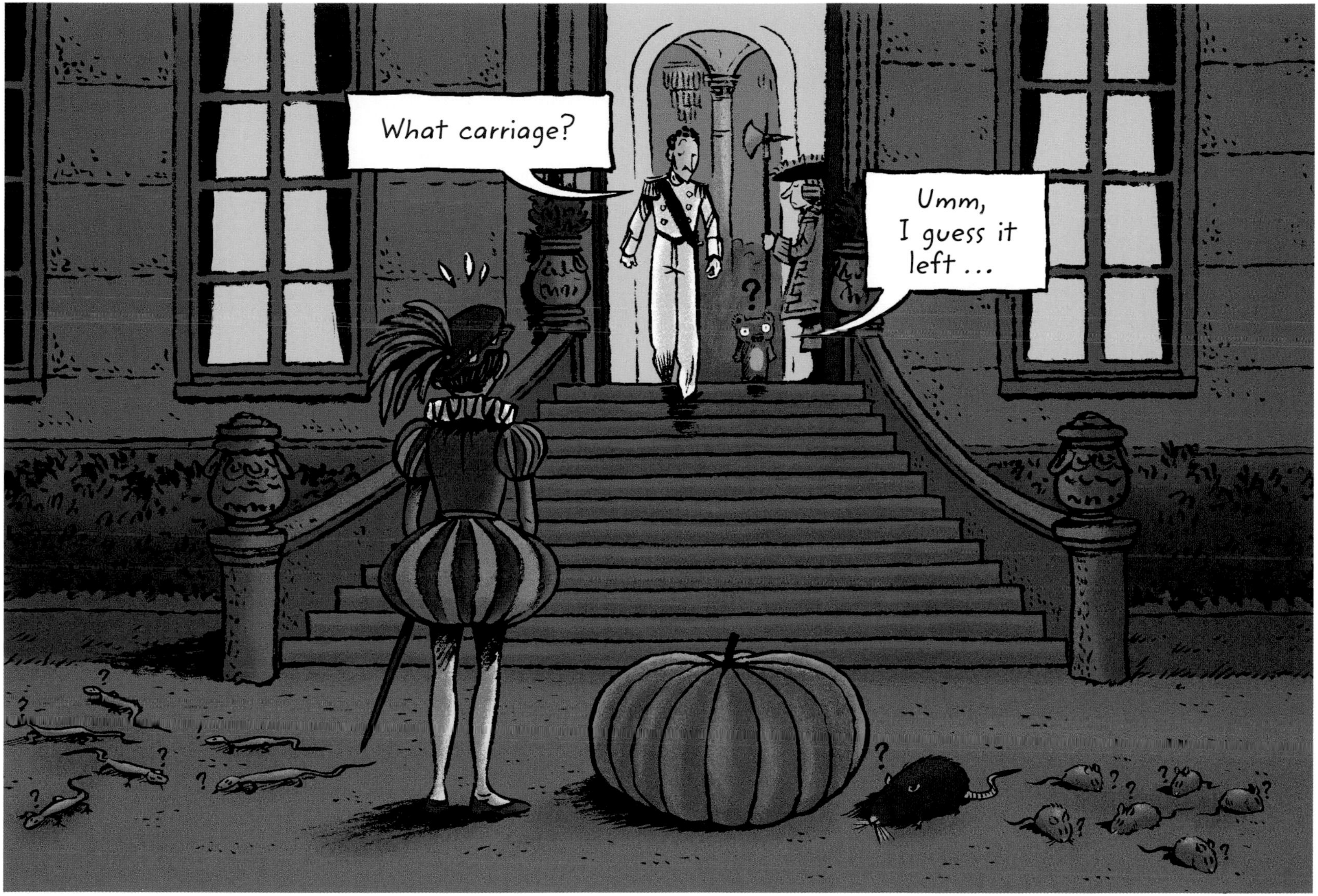
What carriage?
Umm, I guess it left ...

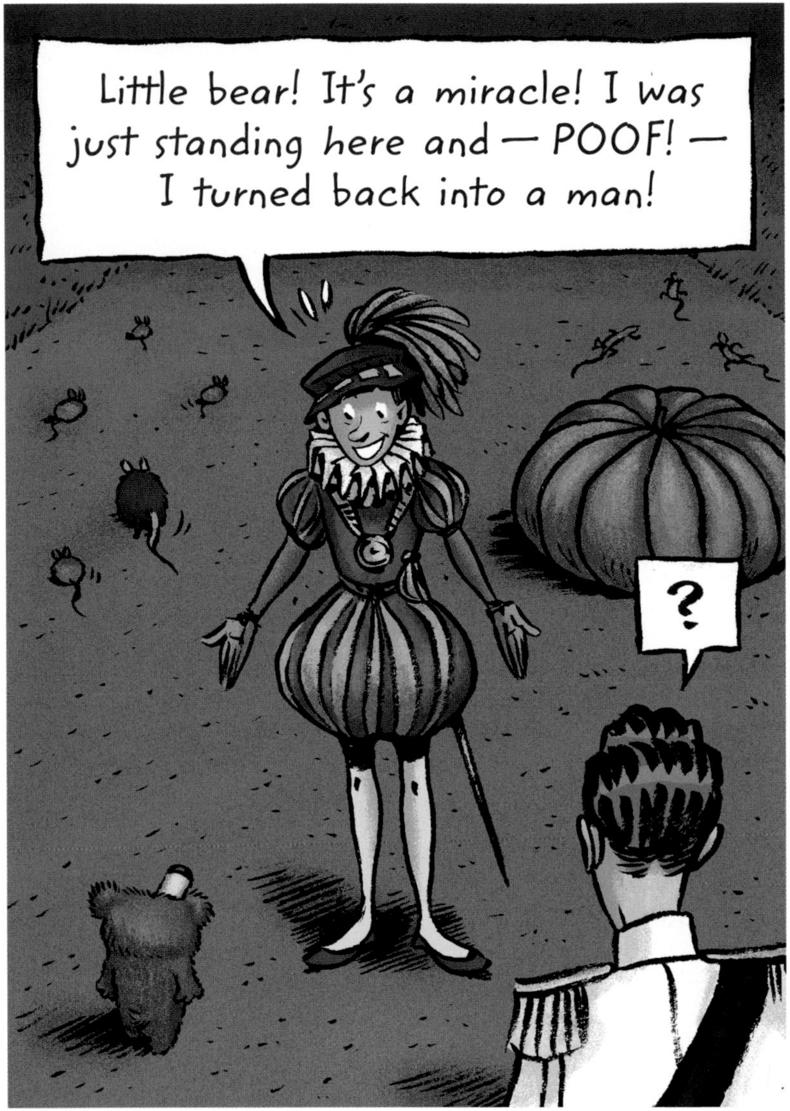
Little bear! It's a miracle! I was just standing here and — POOF! — I turned back into a man!
?

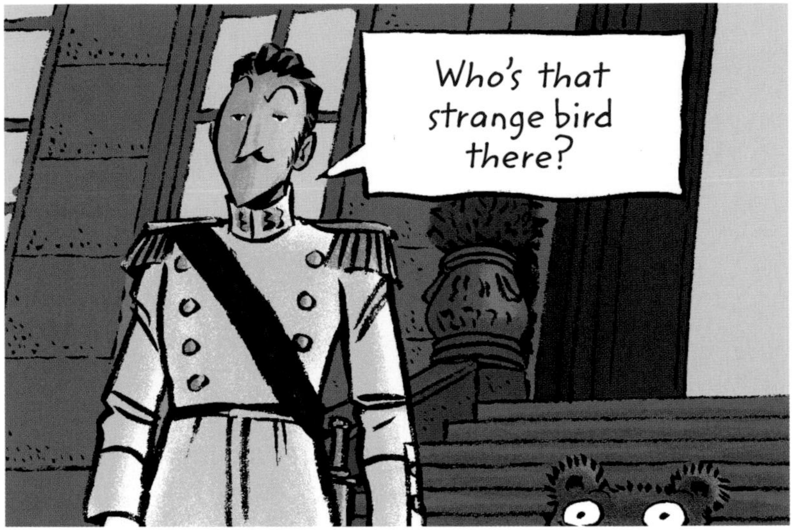
Who's that strange bird there?

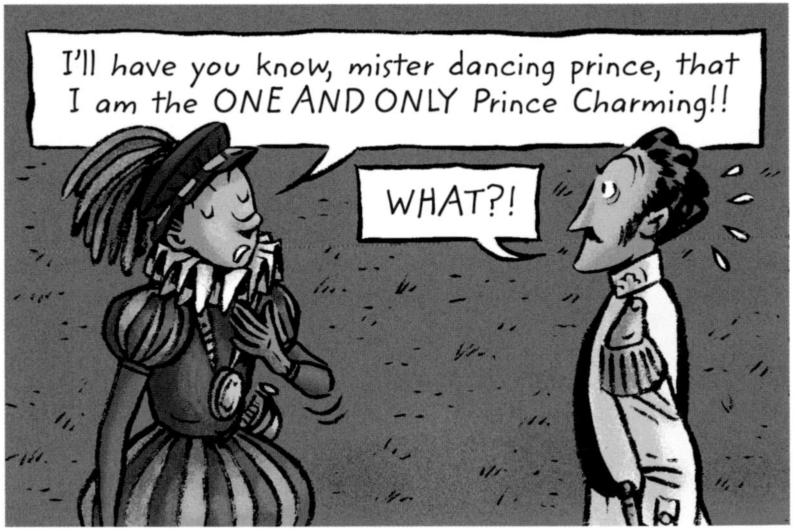
I'll have you know, mister dancing prince, that I am the ONE AND ONLY Prince Charming!!
WHAT?!

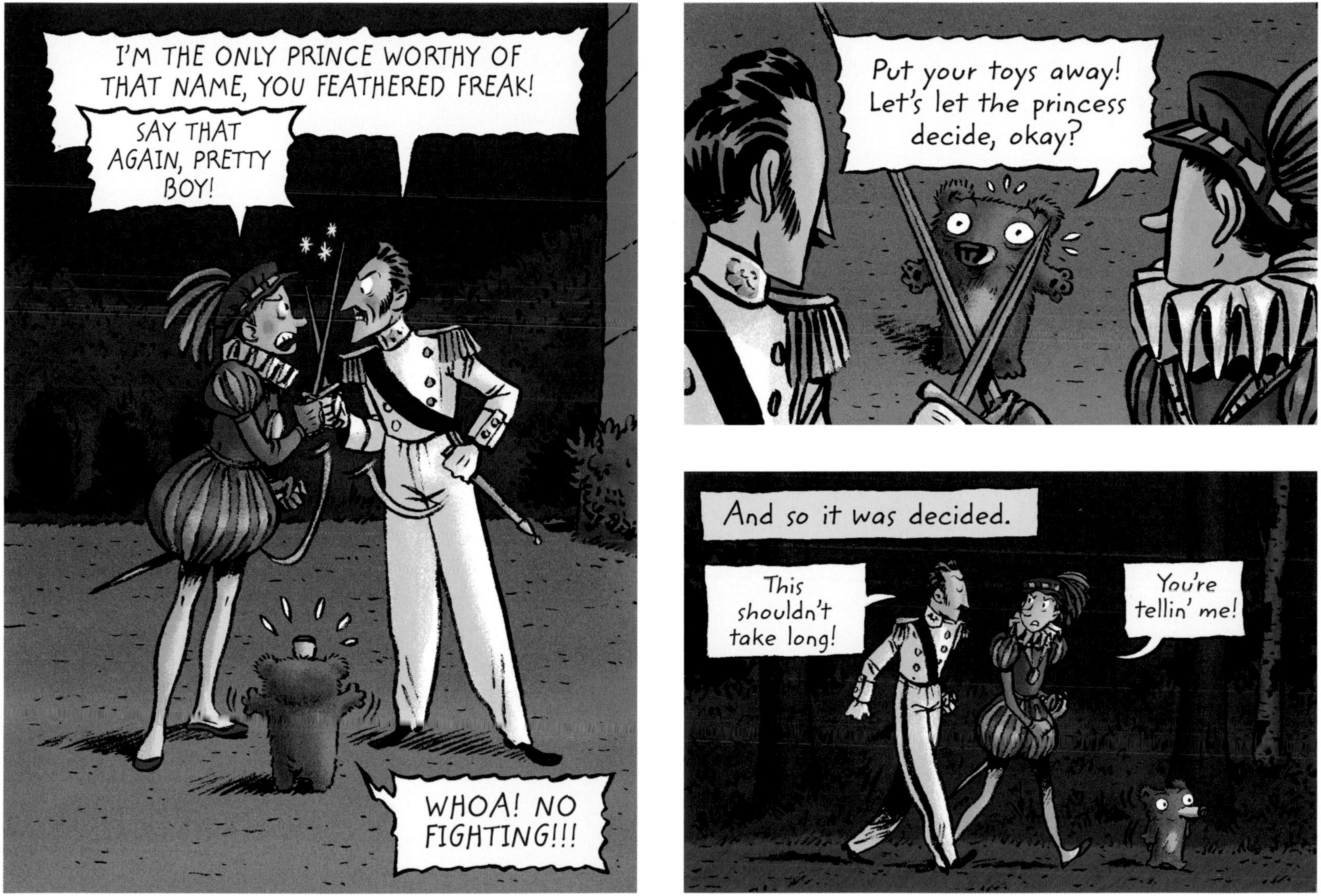
I'M THE ONLY PRINCE WORTHY OF THAT NAME, YOU FEATHERED FREAK!
SAY THAT AGAIN, PRETTY BOY!
WHOA! NO FIGHTING!!!
Put your toys away! Let's let the princess decide, okay?
And so it was decided.
This shouldn't take long!
You're tellin' me!

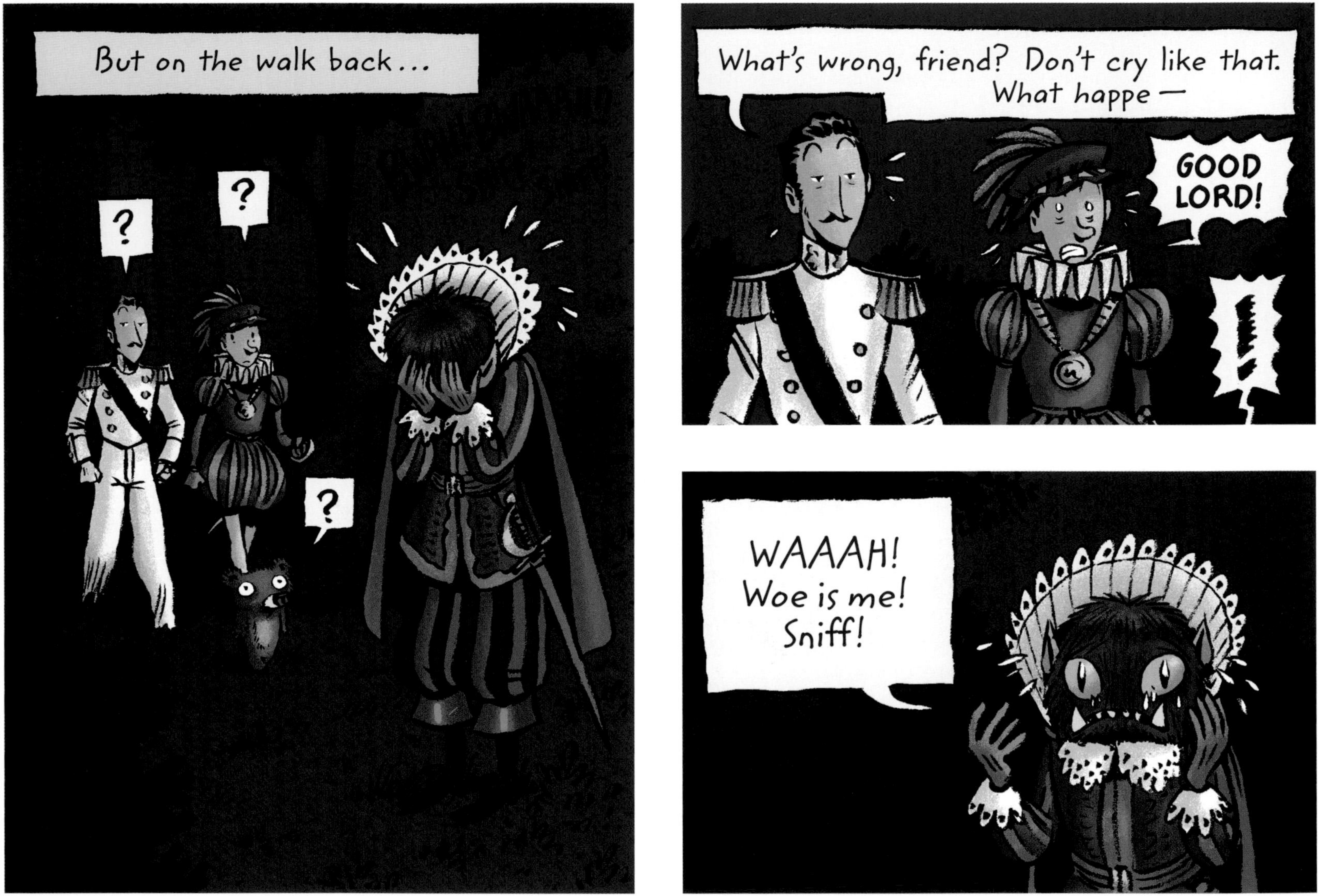
But on the walk back...
?
?
?
What's wrong, friend? Don't cry like that. What happe—
GOOD LORD!
!
WAAAH! Woe is me! Sniff!

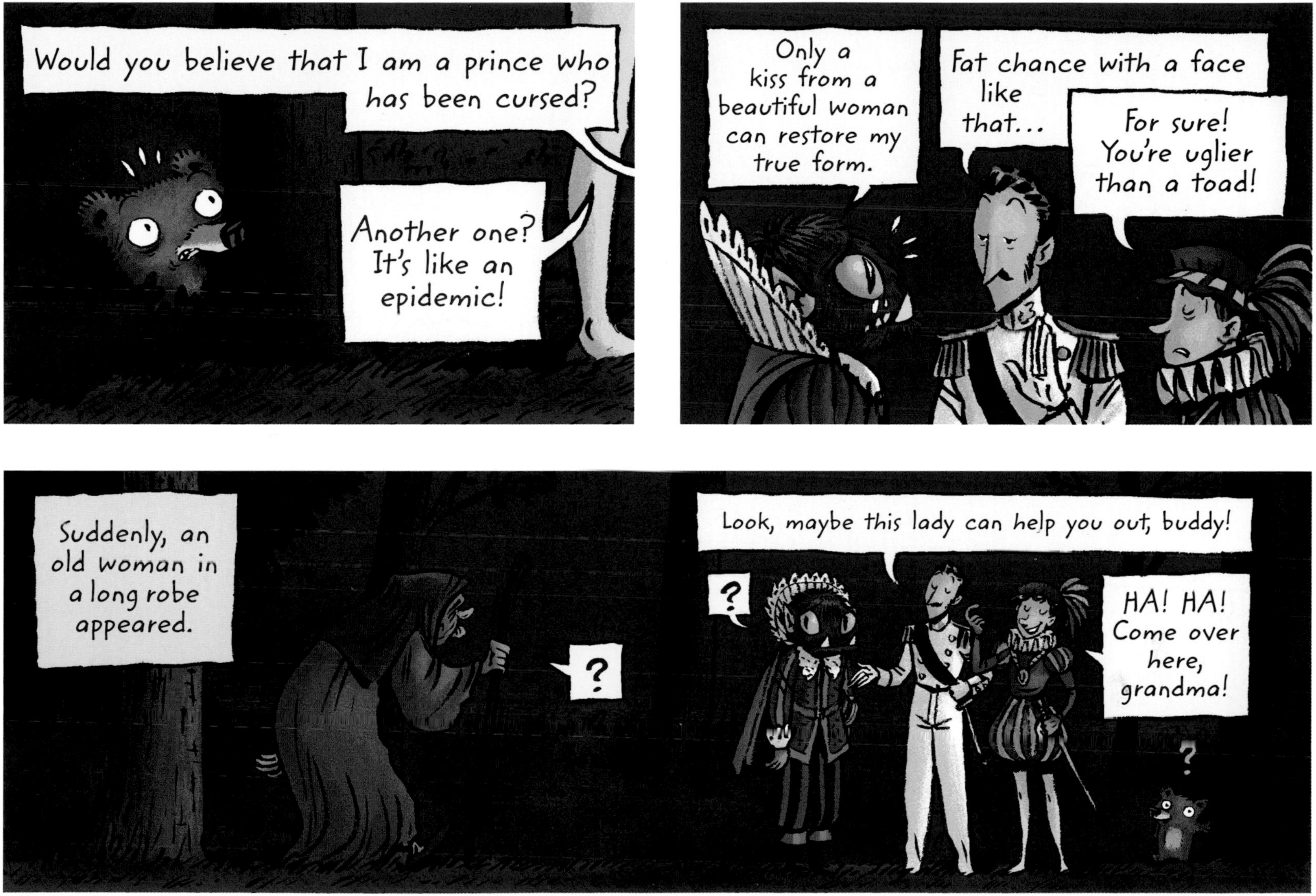
Would you believe that I am a prince who has been cursed?
Another one? It's like an epidemic!
Only a kiss from a beautiful woman can restore my true form.
Fat chance with a face like that...
For sure! You're uglier than a toad!
Suddenly, an old woman in a long robe appeared.
?
Look, maybe this lady can help you out, buddy!
?
HA! HA! Come over here, grandma!
?

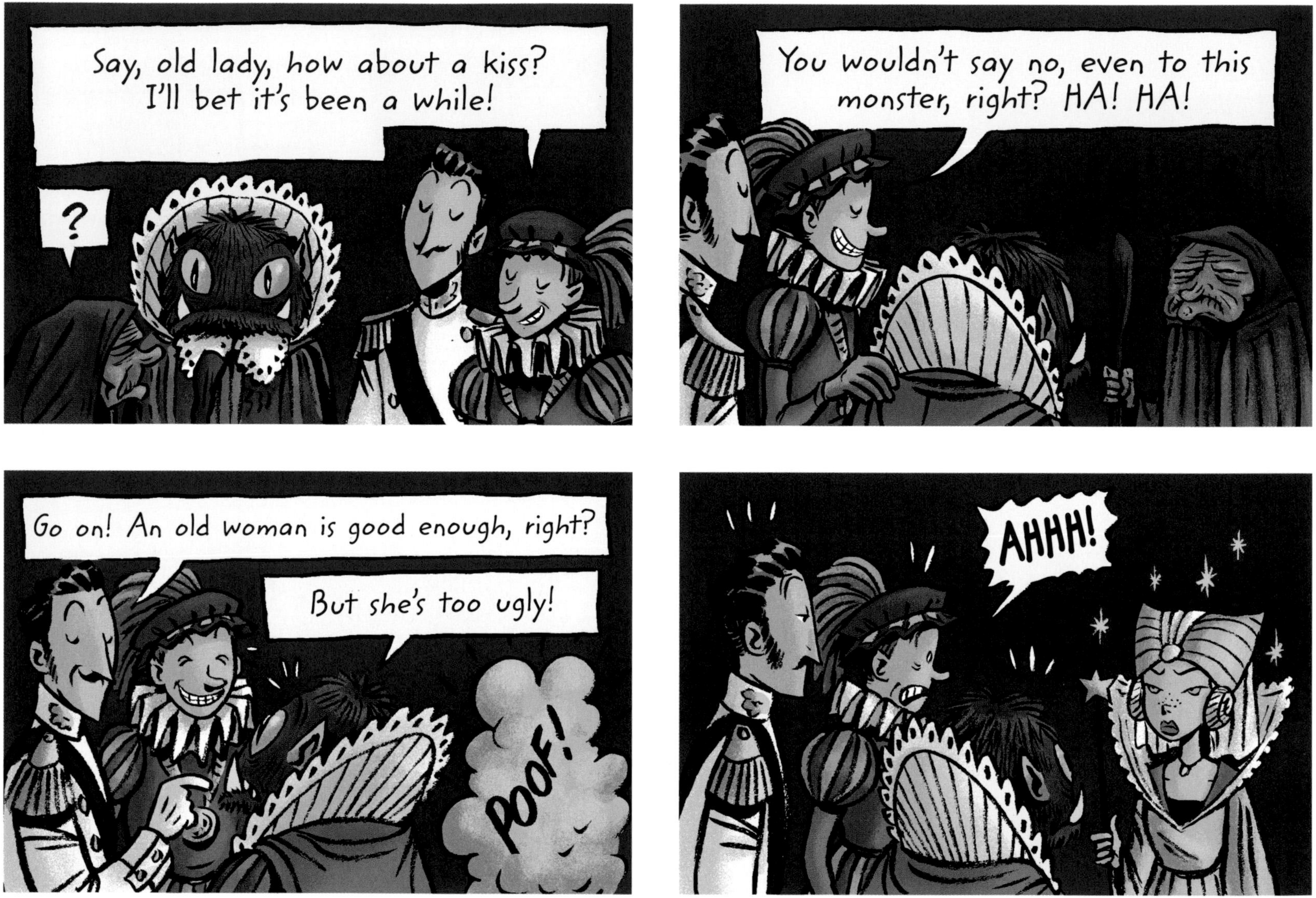
Say, old lady, how about a kiss? I'll bet it's been a while!
?
You wouldn't say no, even to this monster, right? HA! HA!
Go on! An old woman is good enough, right?
But she's too ugly!
POOF!
AHHH!

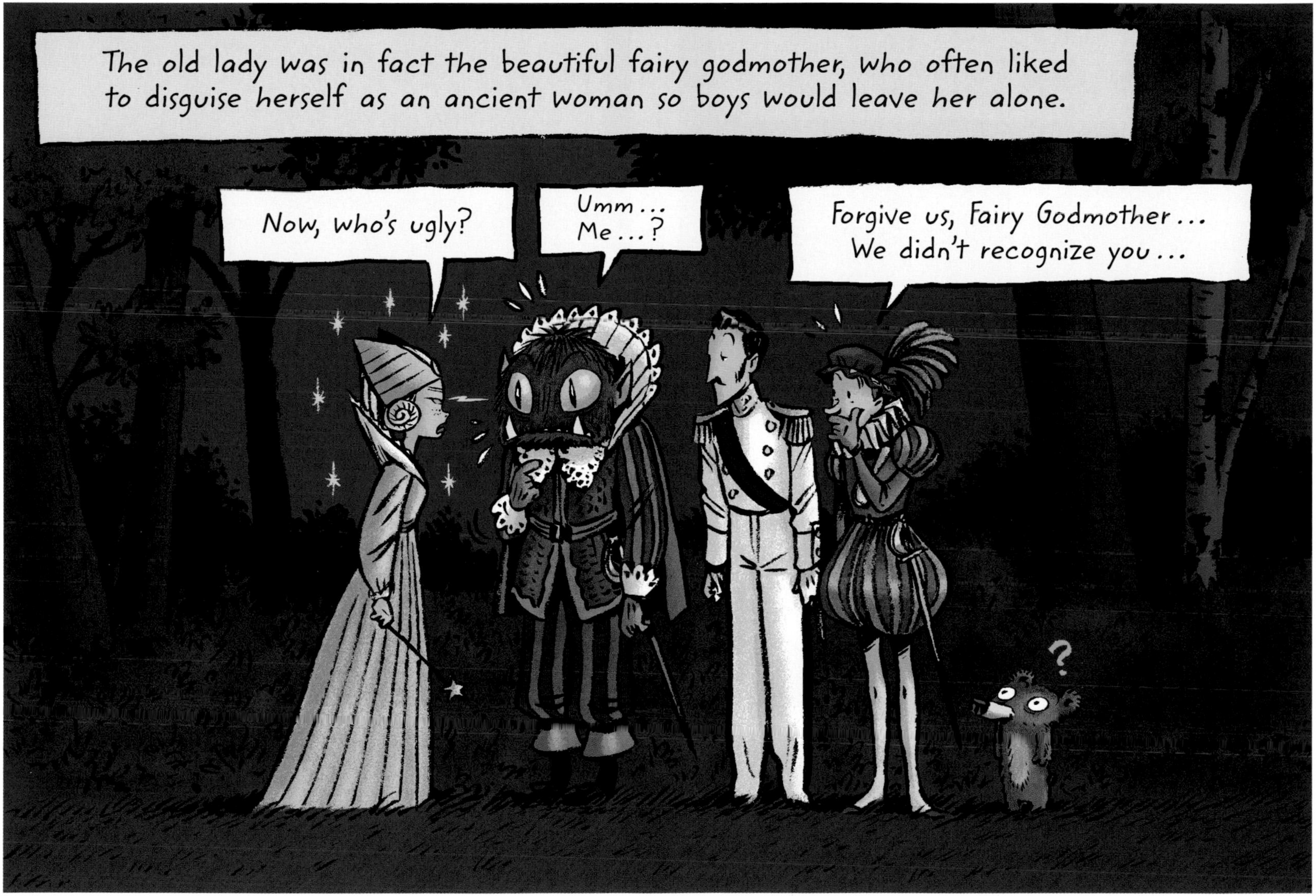
The old lady was in fact the beautiful fairy godmother, who often liked to disguise herself as an ancient woman so boys would leave her alone.
Now, who's ugly?
Umm... Me...?
Forgive us, Fairy Godmother... We didn't recognize you...
?

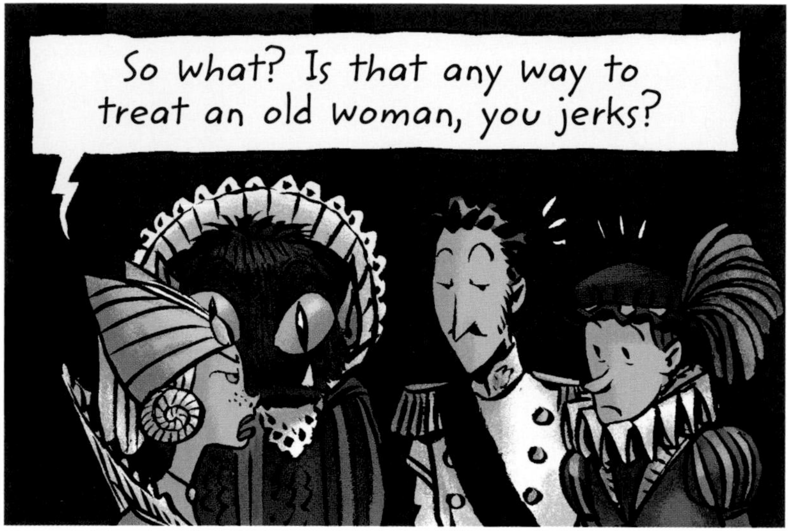
So what? Is that any way to treat an old woman, you jerks?

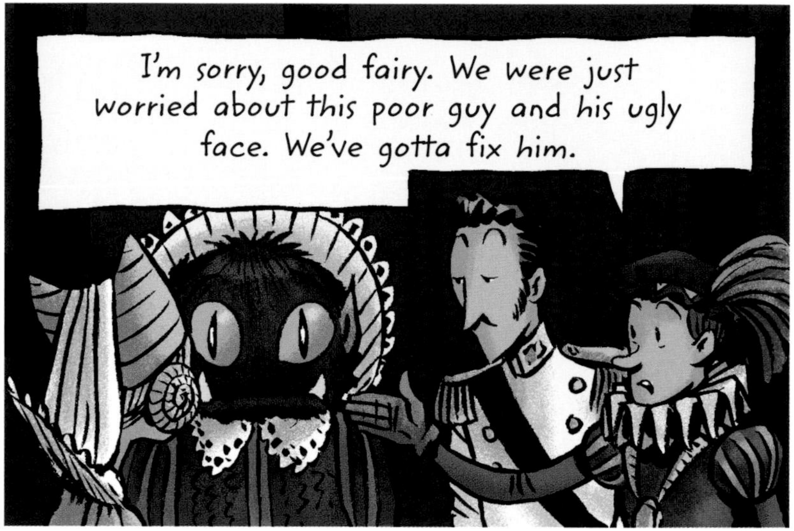
I'm sorry, good fairy. We were just worried about this poor guy and his ugly face. We've gotta fix him.

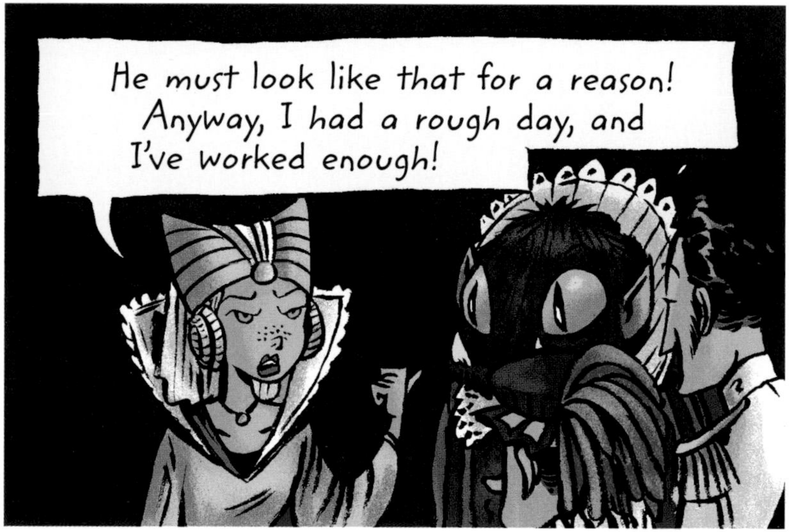
He must look like that for a reason! Anyway, I had a rough day, and I've worked enough!

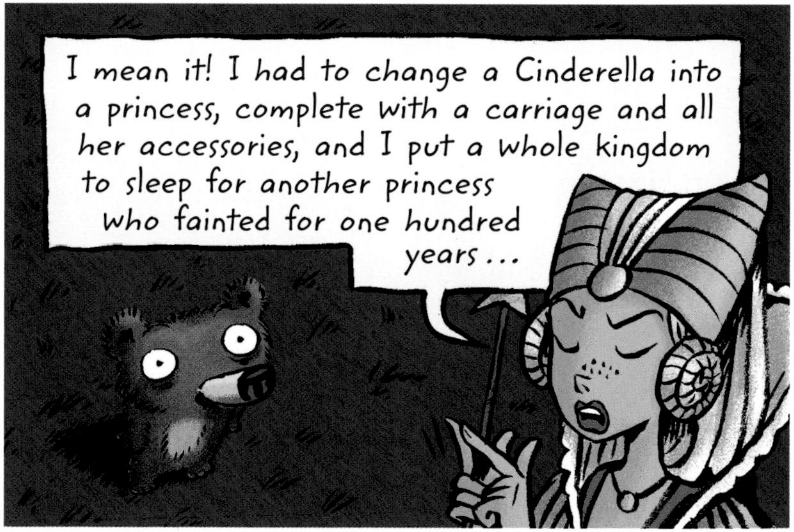
I mean it! I had to change a Cinderella into a princess, complete with a carriage and all her accessories, and I put a whole kingdom to sleep for another princess who fainted for one hundred years...

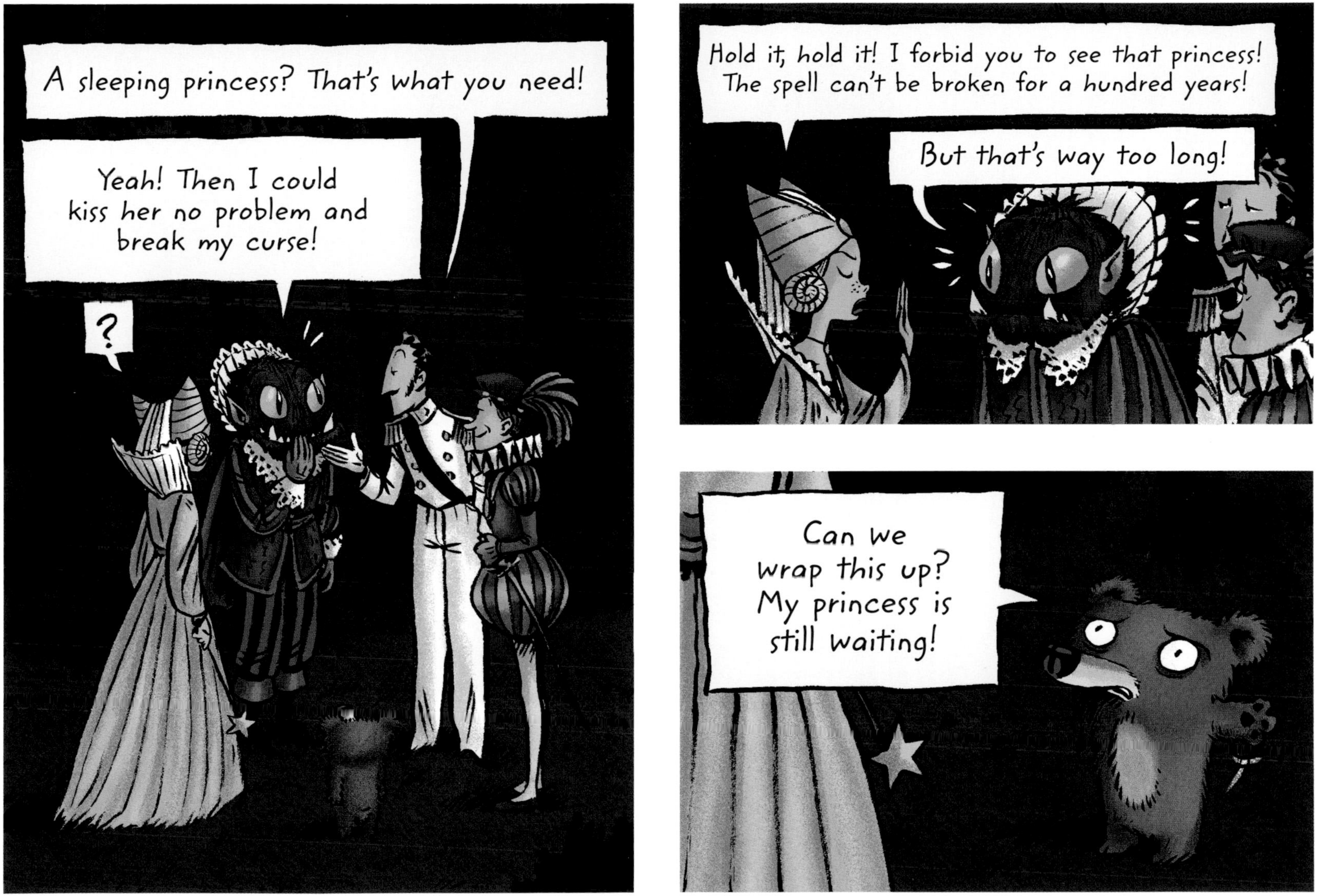
A sleeping princess? That's what you need!
Yeah! Then I could kiss her no problem and break my curse!
?
Hold it, hold it! I forbid you to see that princess! The spell can't be broken for a hundred years!
But that's way too long!
Can we wrap this up? My princess is still waiting!

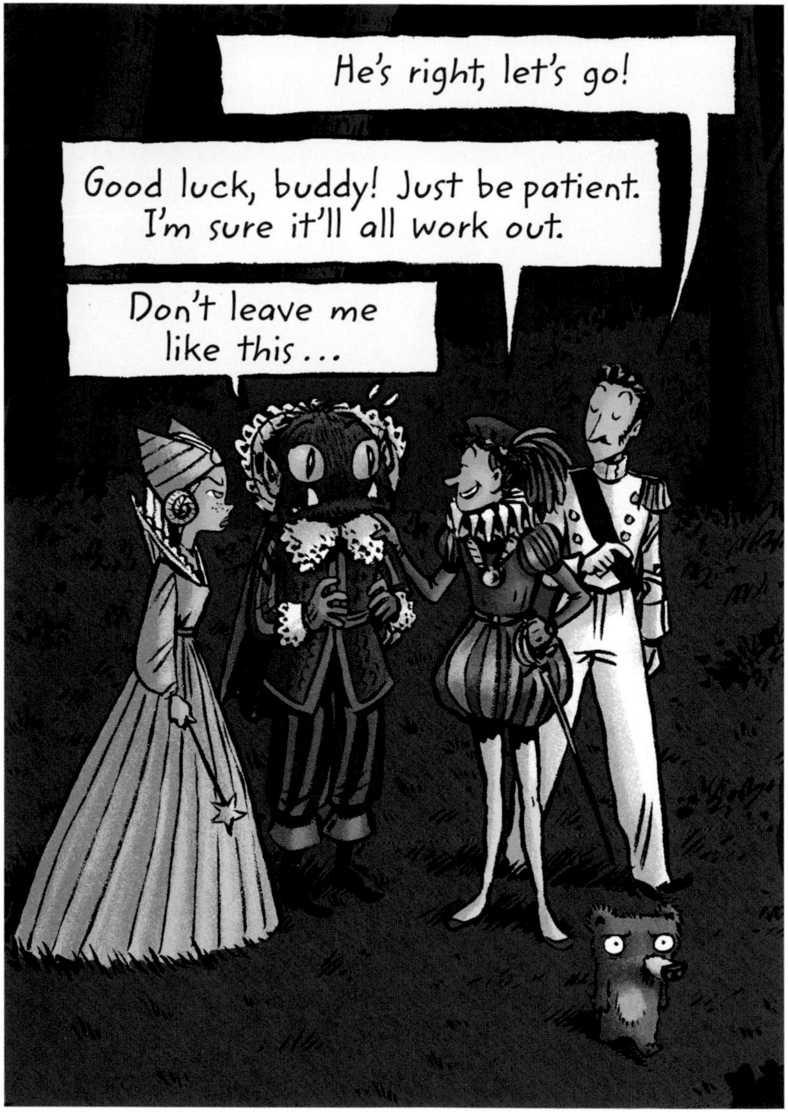
He's right, let's go!
Good luck, buddy! Just be patient. I'm sure it'll all work out.
Don't leave me like this . . .

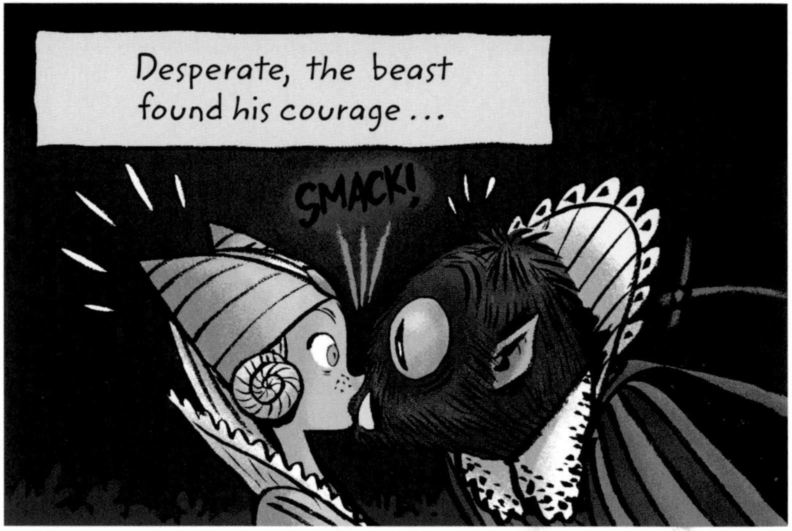
Desperate, the beast found his courage . . .
SMACK!

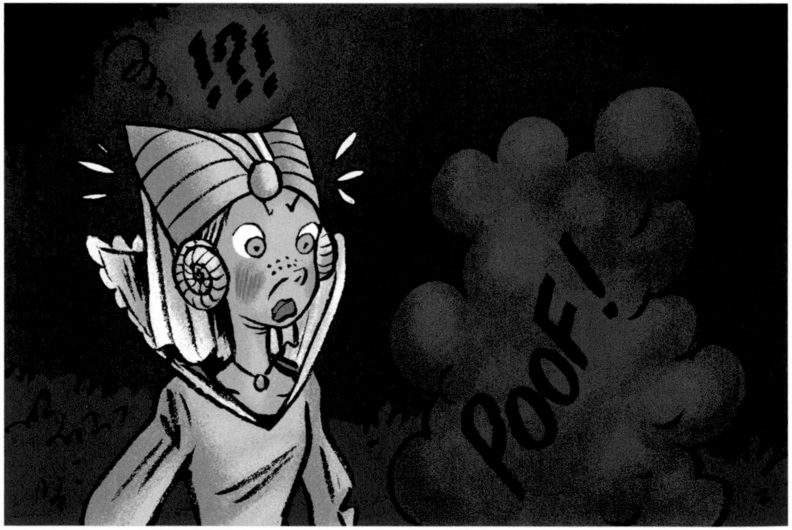
!?!
POOF!

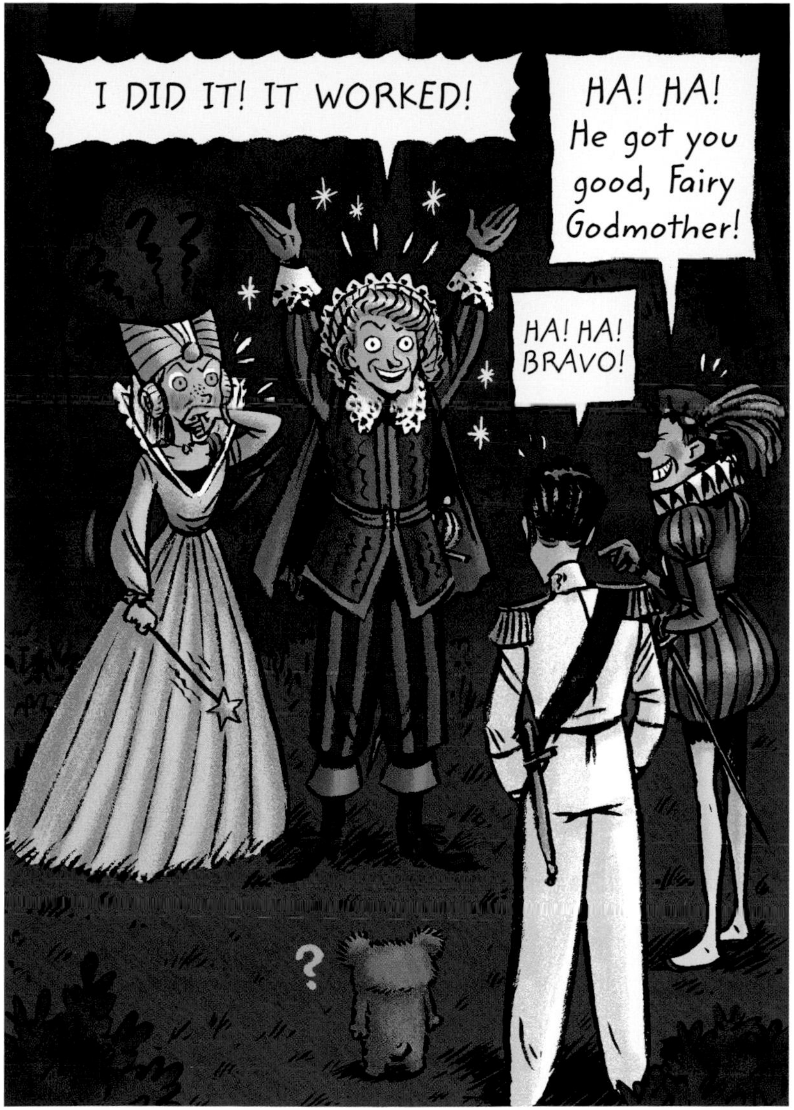
I DID IT! IT WORKED!
HA! HA! He got you good, Fairy Godmother!
HA! HA! BRAVO!
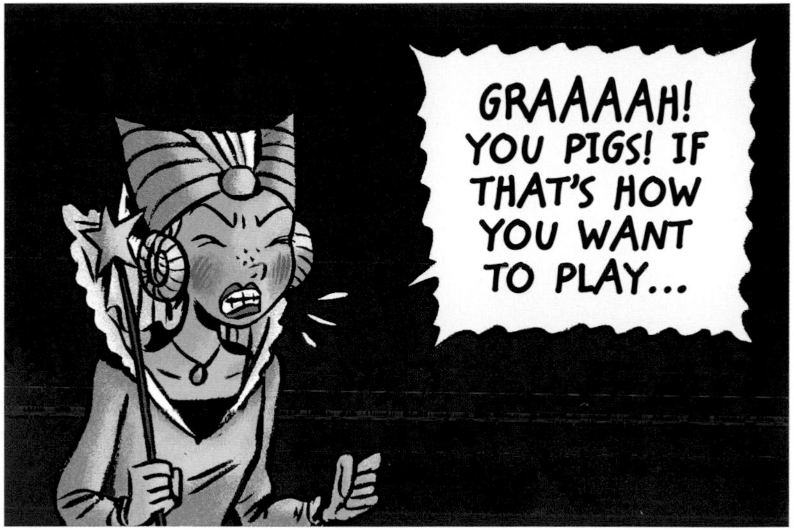
GRAAAAH! YOU PIGS! IF THAT'S HOW YOU WANT TO PLAY...
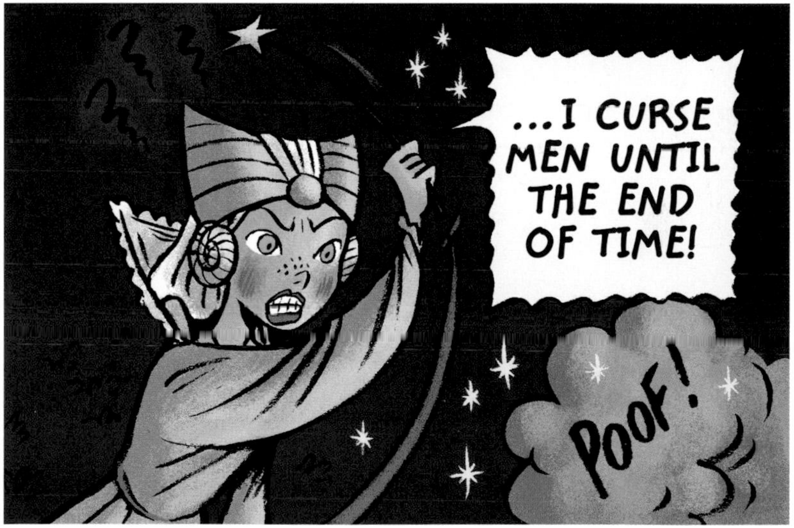
...I CURSE MEN UNTIL THE END OF TIME!
POOF!

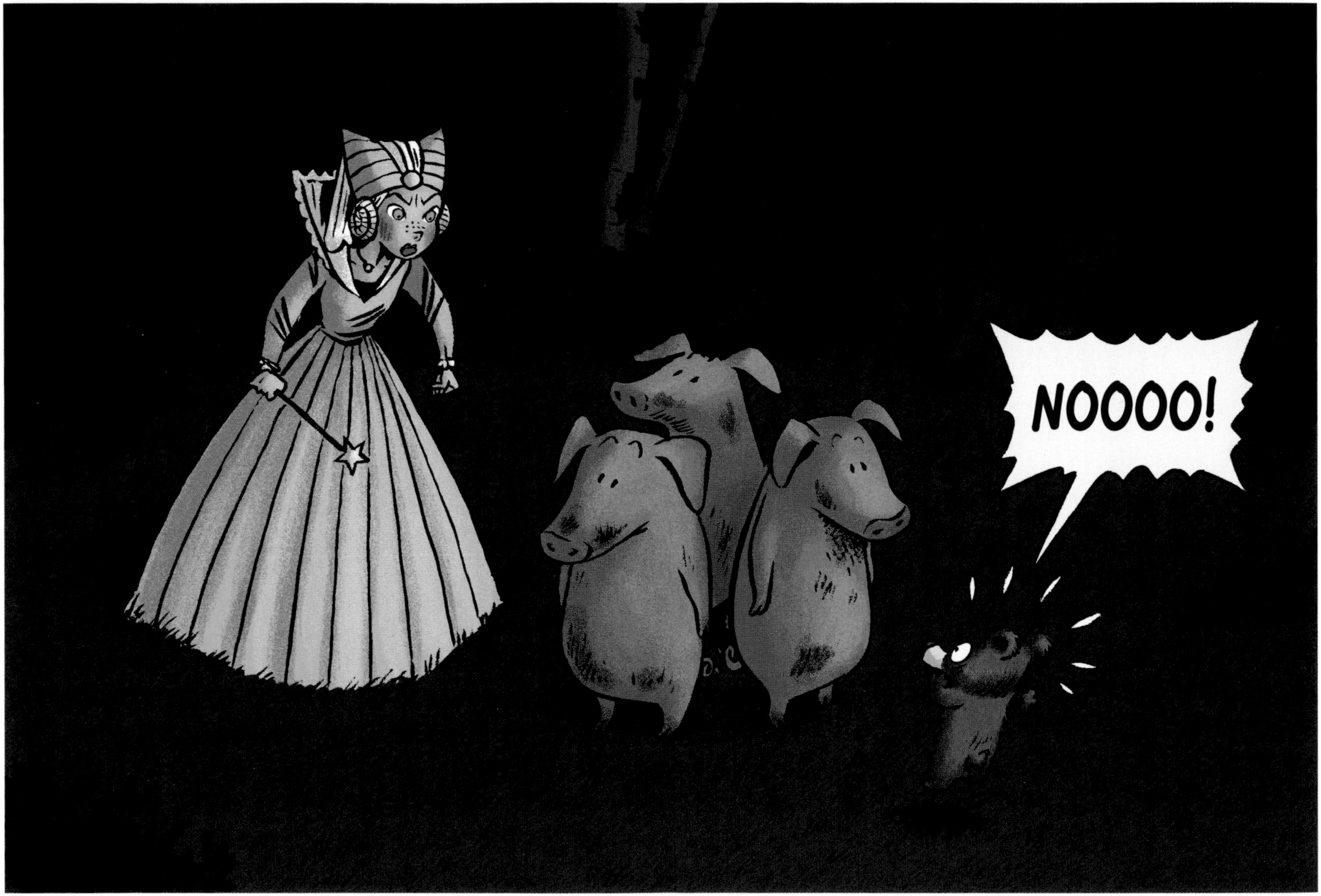
NOOOO!

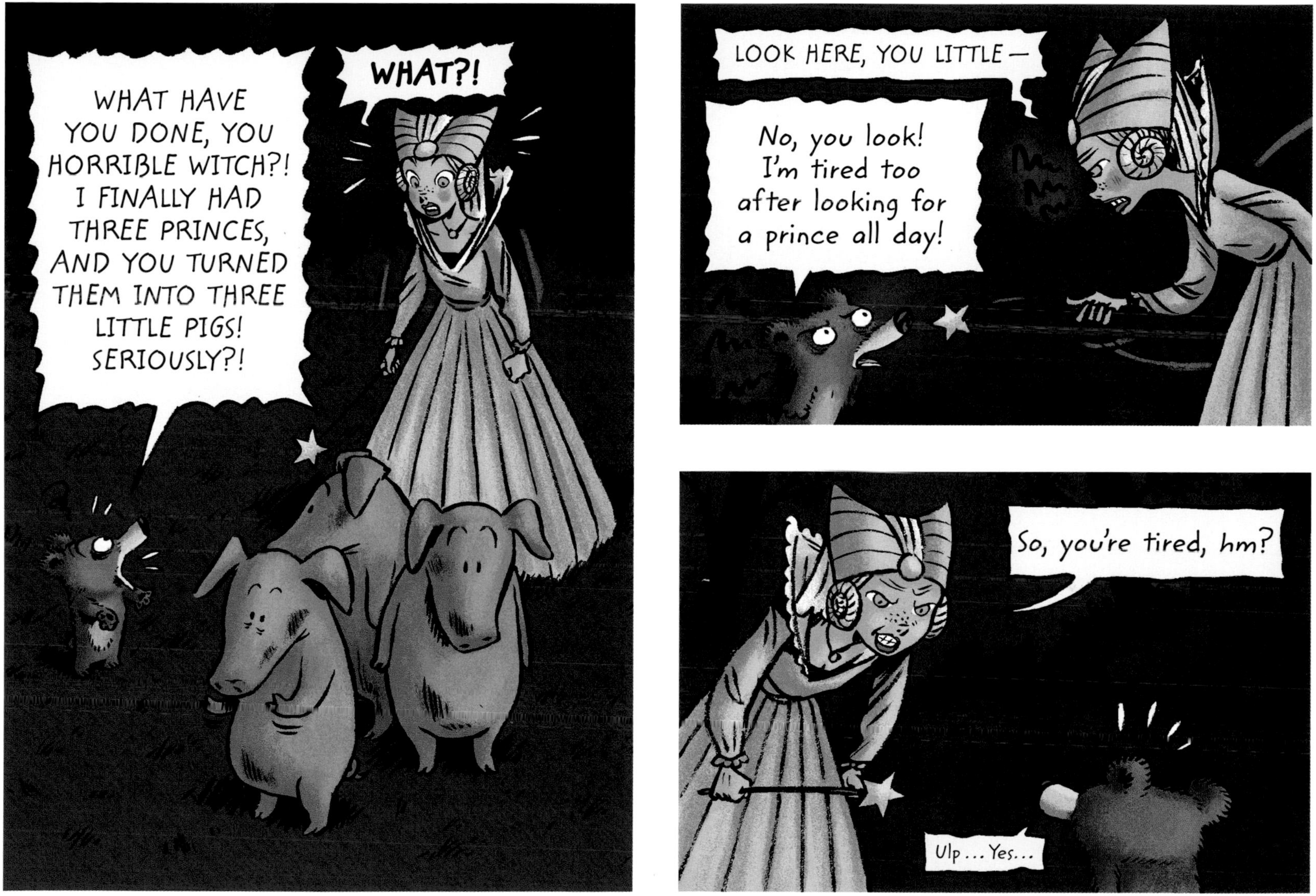
WHAT HAVE YOU DONE, YOU HORRIBLE WITCH?! I FINALLY HAD THREE PRINCES, AND YOU TURNED THEM INTO THREE LITTLE PIGS! SERIOUSLY?!
WHAT?!
LOOK HERE, YOU LITTLE—
No, you look! I'm tired too after looking for a prince all day!
So, you're tired, hm?
Ulp... Yes...

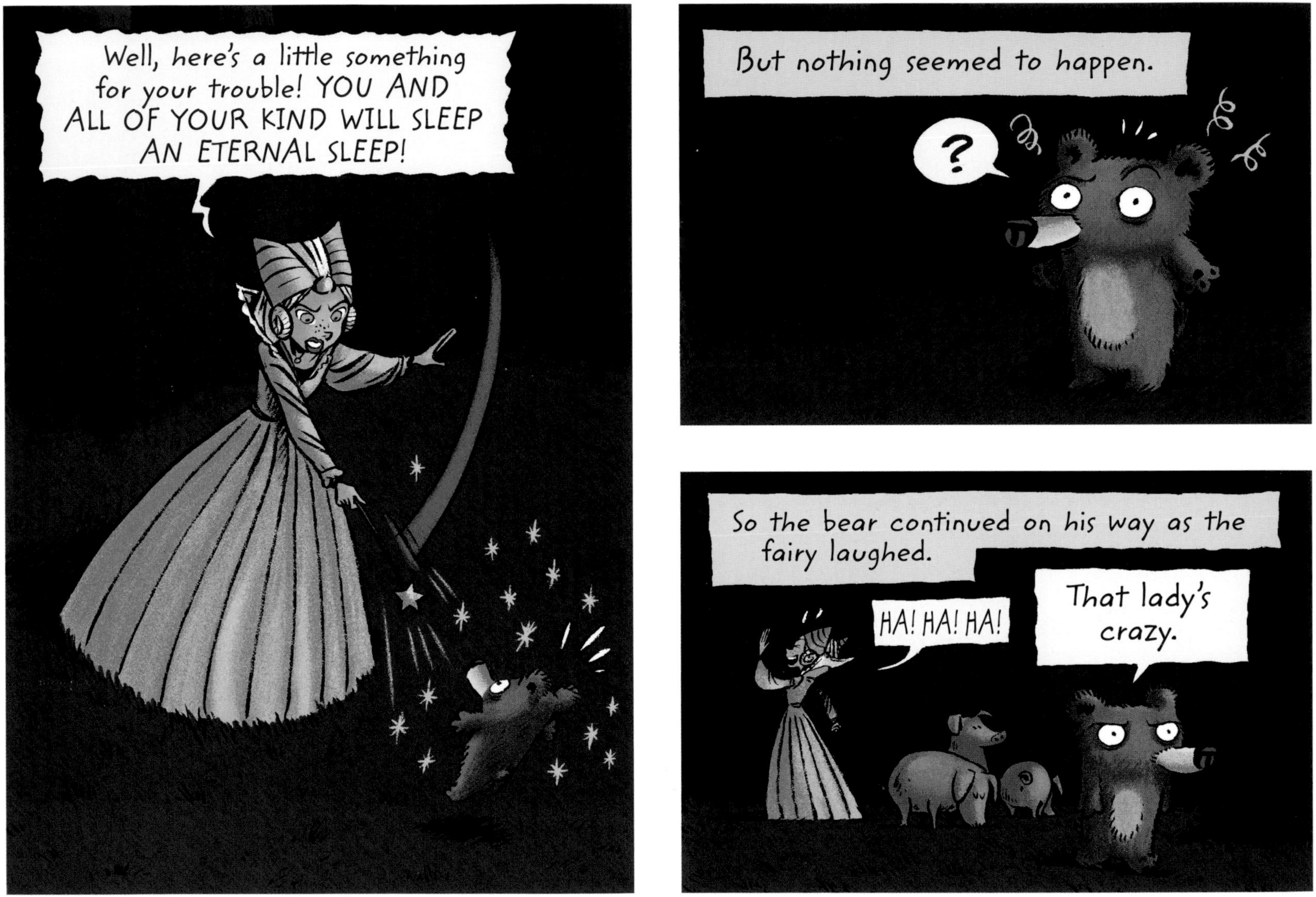
Well, here's a little something for your trouble! YOU AND ALL OF YOUR KIND WILL SLEEP AN ETERNAL SLEEP!
But nothing seemed to happen.
?
So the bear continued on his way as the fairy laughed.
HA! HA! HA!
That lady's crazy.

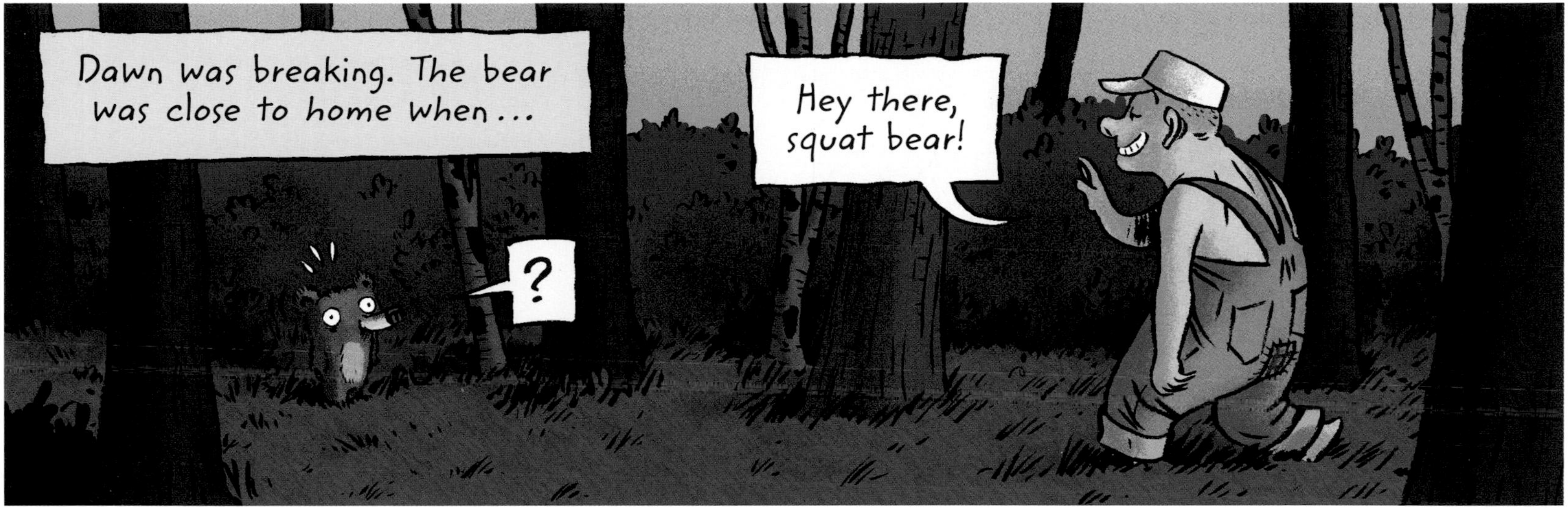
Dawn was breaking. The bear was close to home when...
?
Hey there, squat bear!

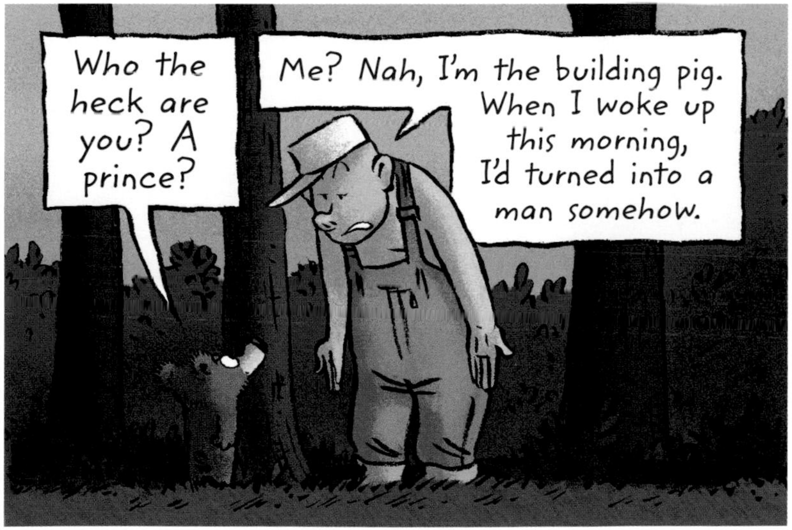
Who the heck are you? A prince?
Me? Nah, I'm the building pig. When I woke up this morning, I'd turned into a man somehow.

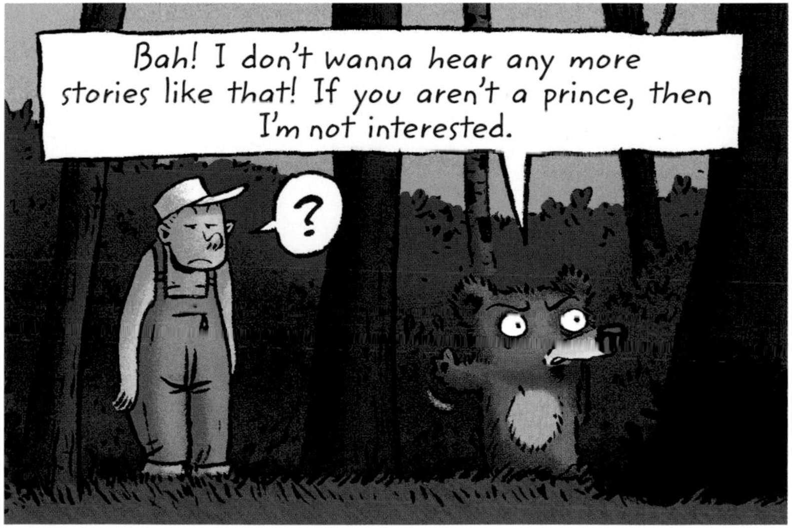
Bah! I don't wanna hear any more stories like that! If you aren't a prince, then I'm not interested.
?

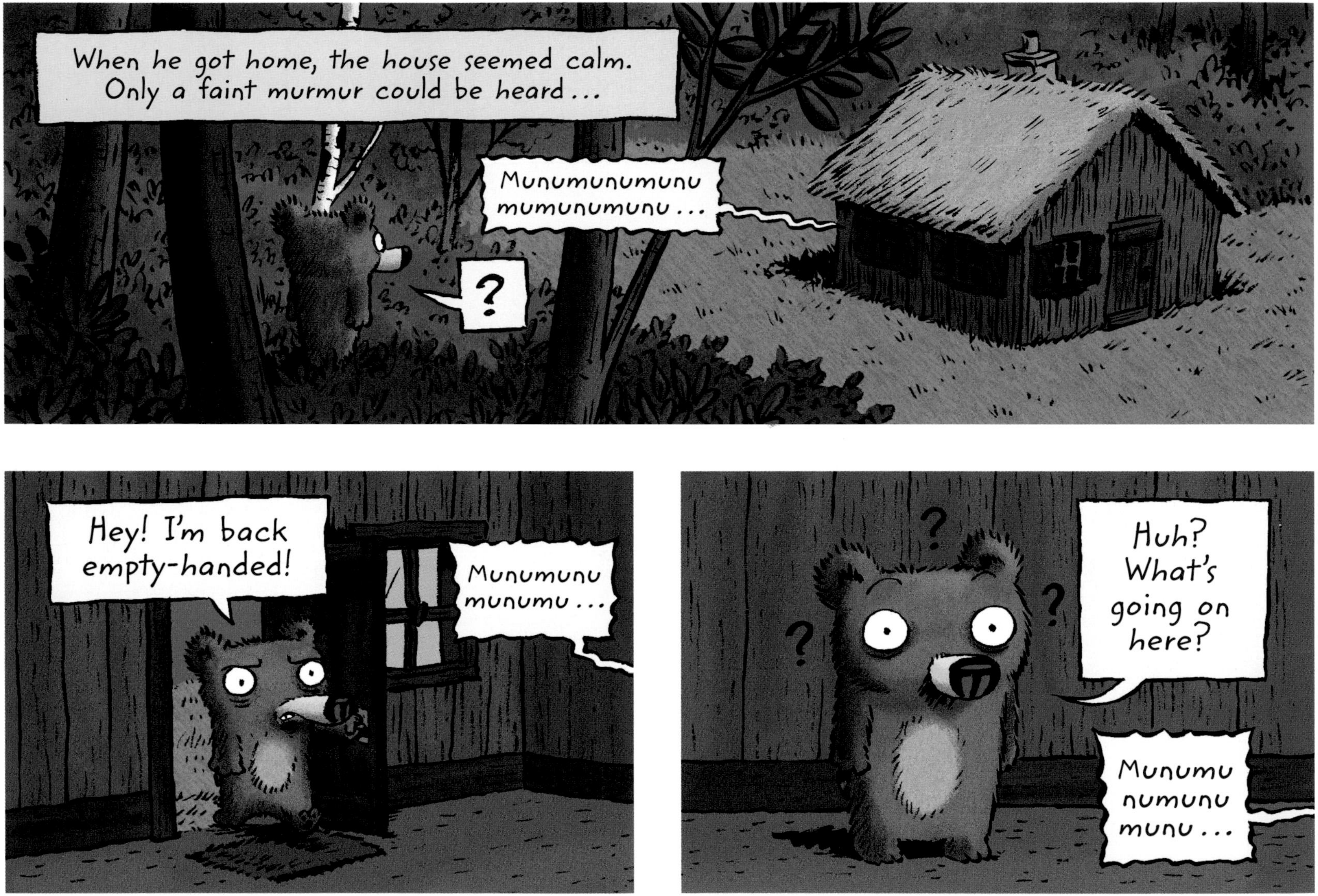
When he got home, the house seemed calm. Only a faint murmur could be heard . . .
Munumunumunu mumunumunu . . .
?
Hey! I'm back empty-handed!
Munumunu munumu . . .
?
?
?
Huh? What's going on here?
Munumu numunu munu . . .

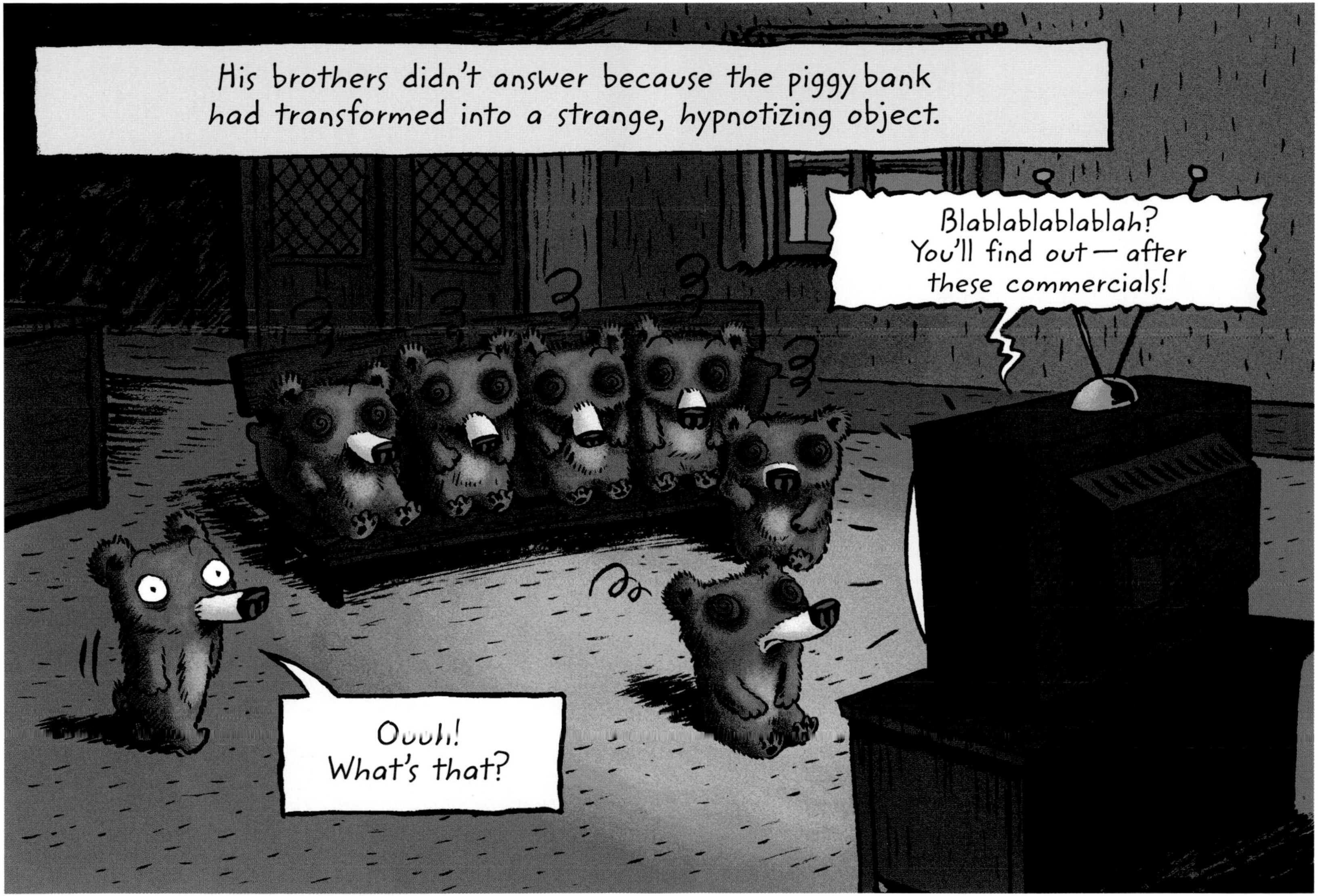
His brothers didn't answer because the piggy bank had transformed into a strange, hypnotizing object.
Blablablablablah? You'll find out — after these commercials!
Oooh! What's that?

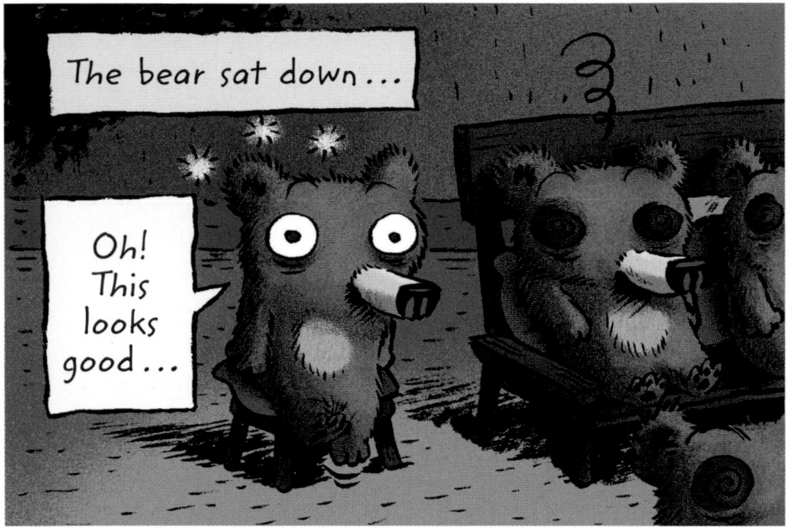
The bear sat down...
Oh! This looks good...

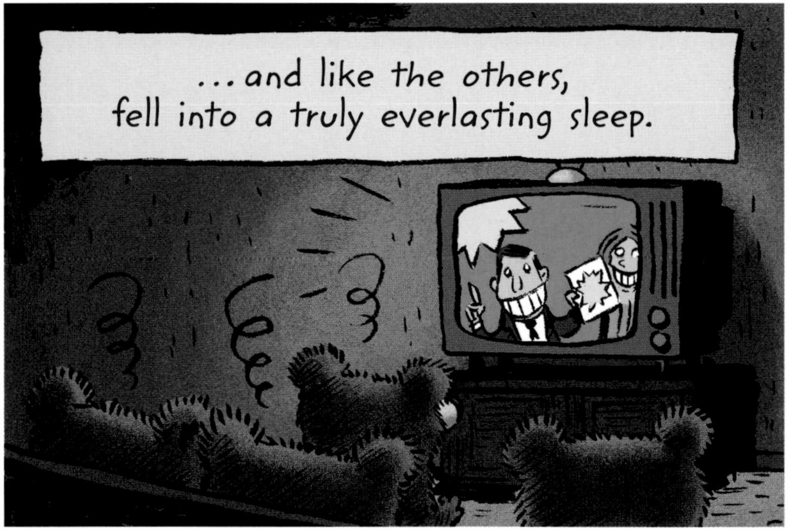
...and like the others, fell into a truly everlasting sleep.

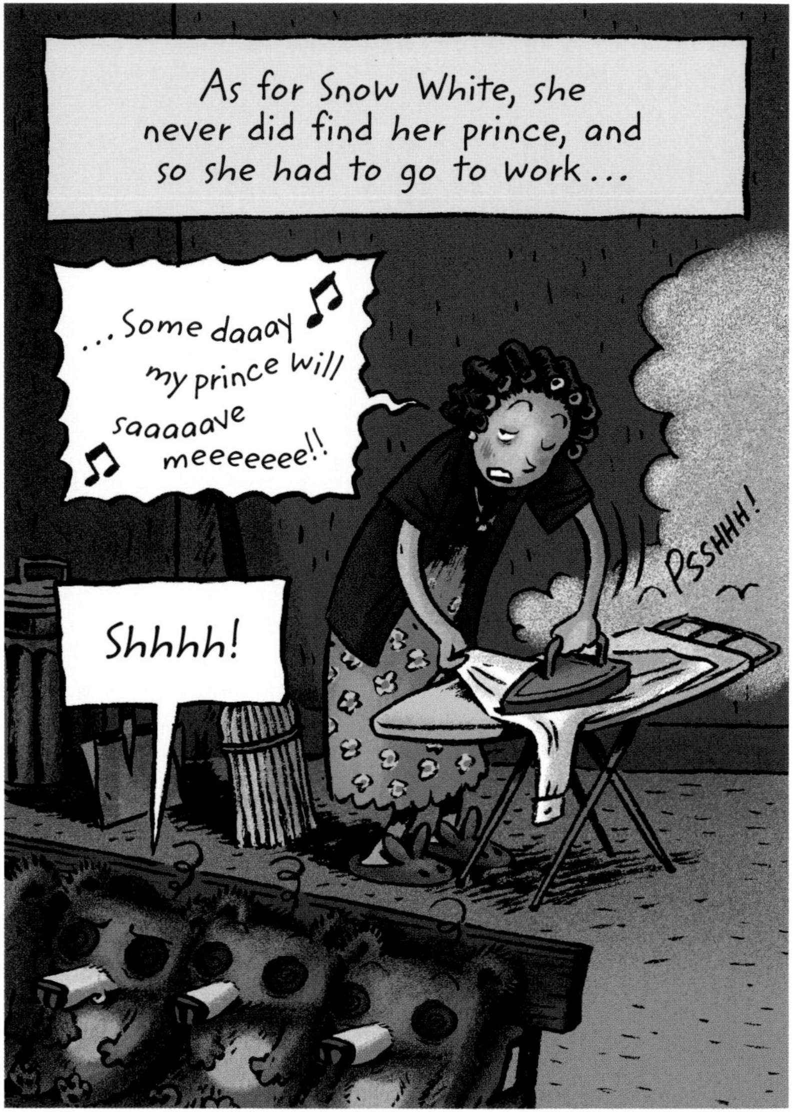
As for Snow White, she never did find her prince, and so she had to go to work...
...Some daaay my prince will saaaaave meeeeeee!!
Shhhh!
PSSHHH!

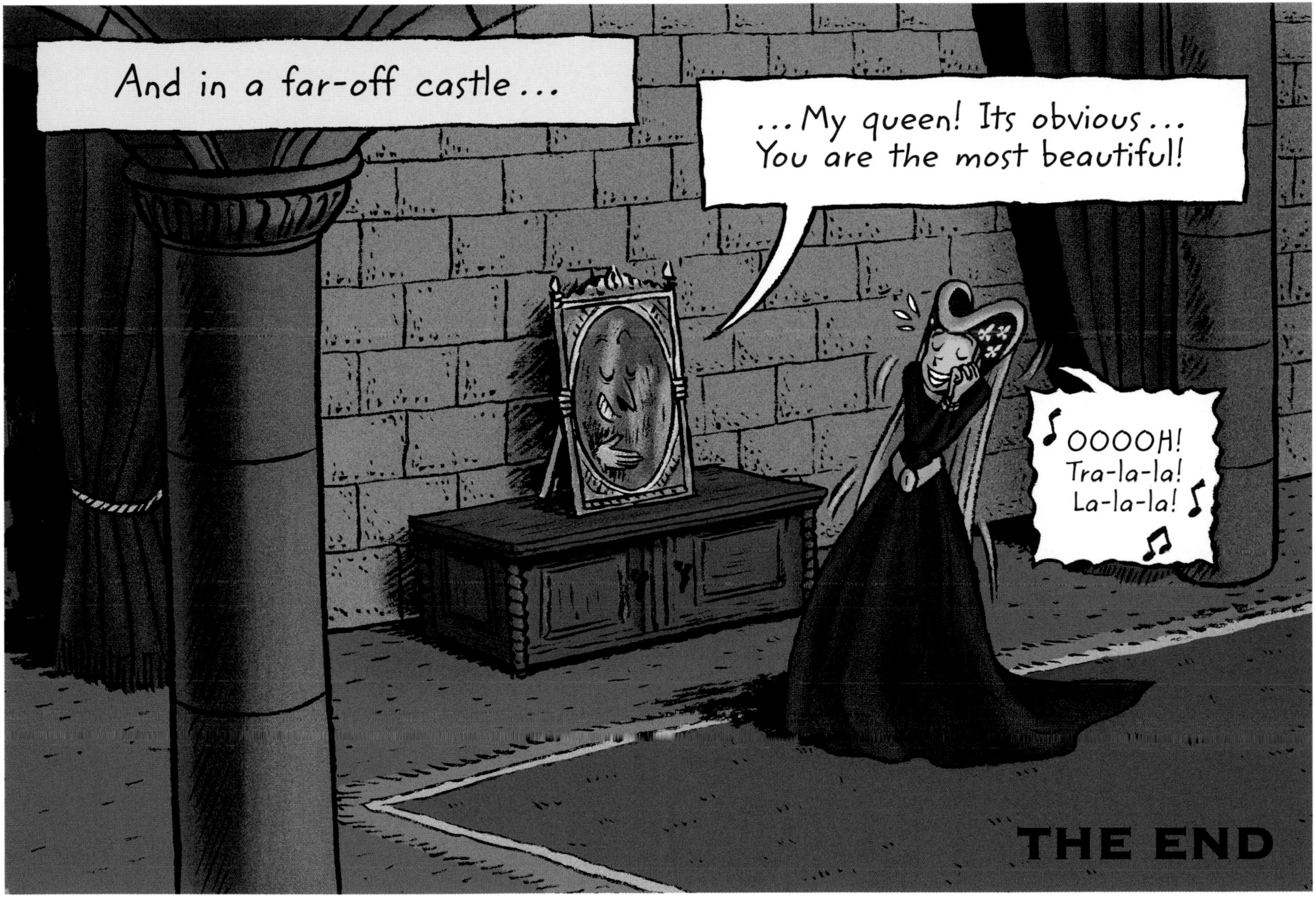
And in a far-off castle...
...My queen! Its obvious...
You are the most beautiful!
OOOOH!
Tra-la-la!
La-la-la!
THE END

BEAUTY AND THE SQUAT BEARS
ÉMILE BRAVO

Translation: J. Gustave McBride

First published in France under the title: *La Belle aux ours nains*
© Editions du Seuil, 2009

English translation © 2011 by Hachette Book Group, Inc.

Yen Press
Hachette Book Group
237 Park Avenue, New York, NY 10017

www.HachetteBookGroup.com
www.YenPress.com

Yen Press is an imprint of Hachette Book Group, Inc.
The Yen Press name and logo are trademarks of
Hachette Book Group, Inc.

First Yen Press Edition: May 2011

ISBN: 978-0-316-08362-1

Library of Congress Control Number: 2010941434

10 9 8 7 6 5 4 3 2 1

RRD/SCP

Printed in China

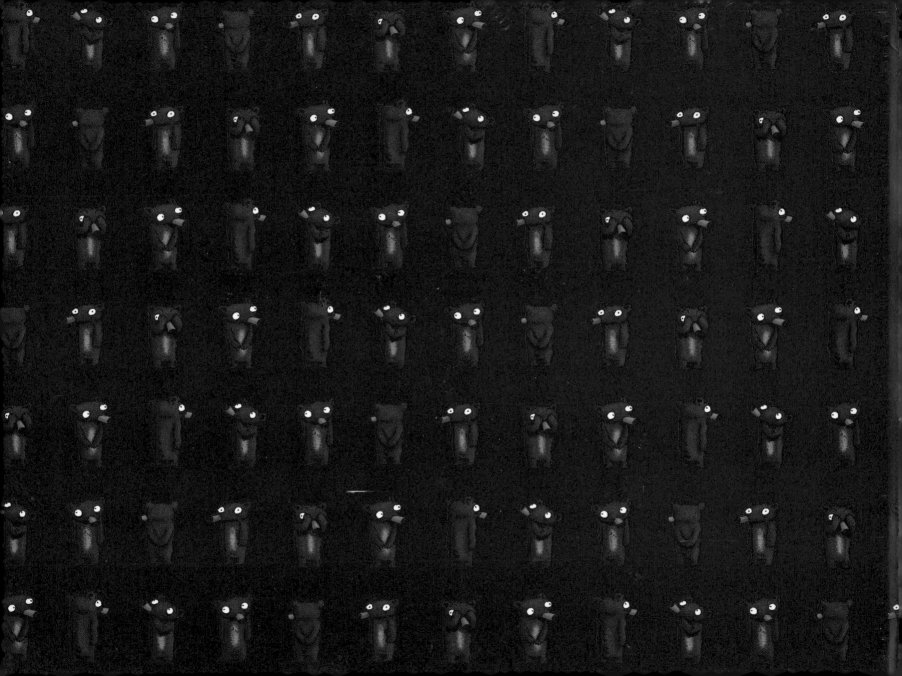

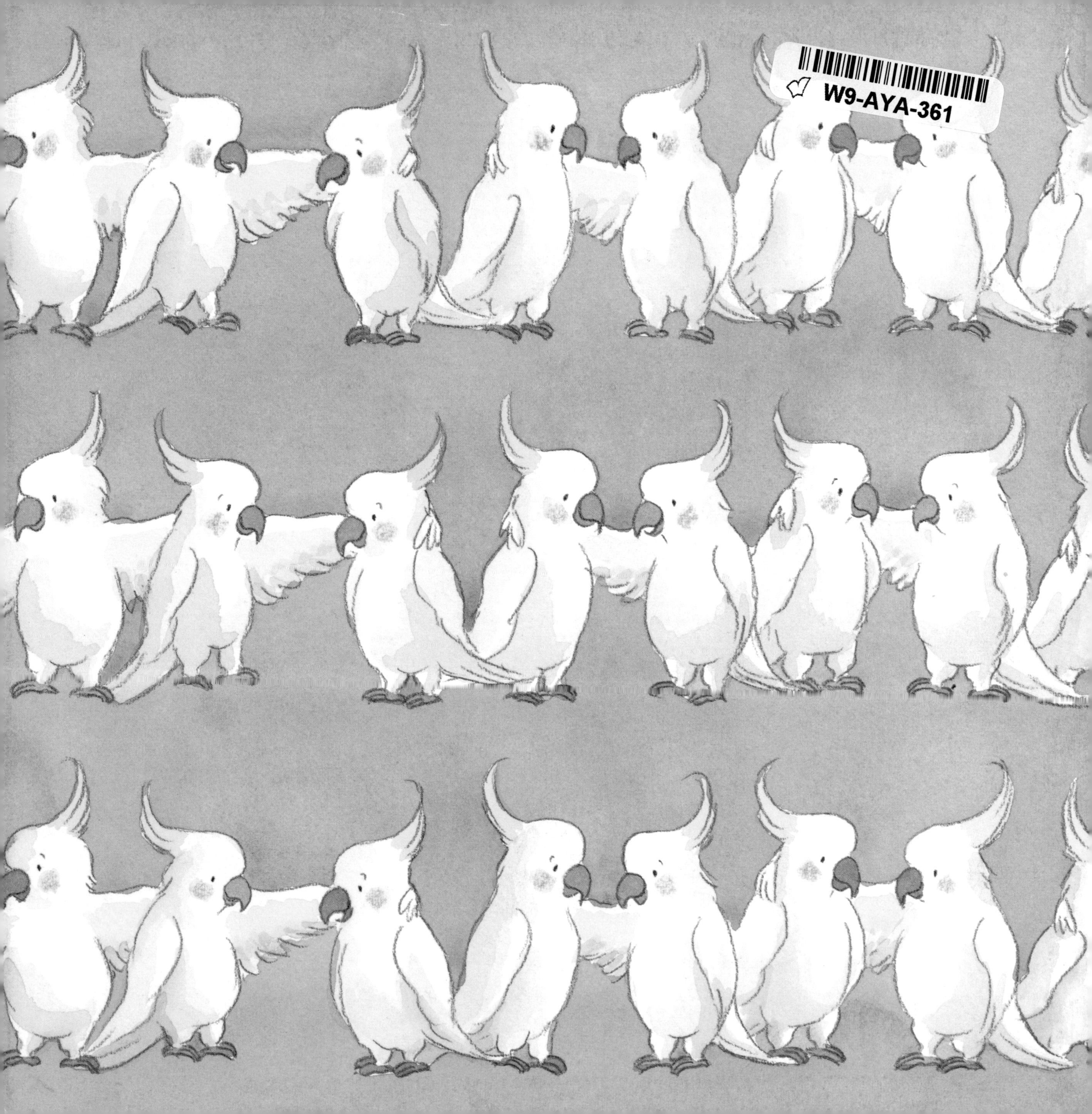

For Benjamin Green

This 2010 edition published by Sandy Creek,
by arrangement with Andersen Press Ltd., London.

Sandy Creek
122 Fifth Avenue
New York, NY 10011

ISBN: 978-1-4351-2303-8

Printed and bound in Singapore
November 2009

1 3 5 7 9 10 8 6 4 2

First published by Andersen Press Ltd., London

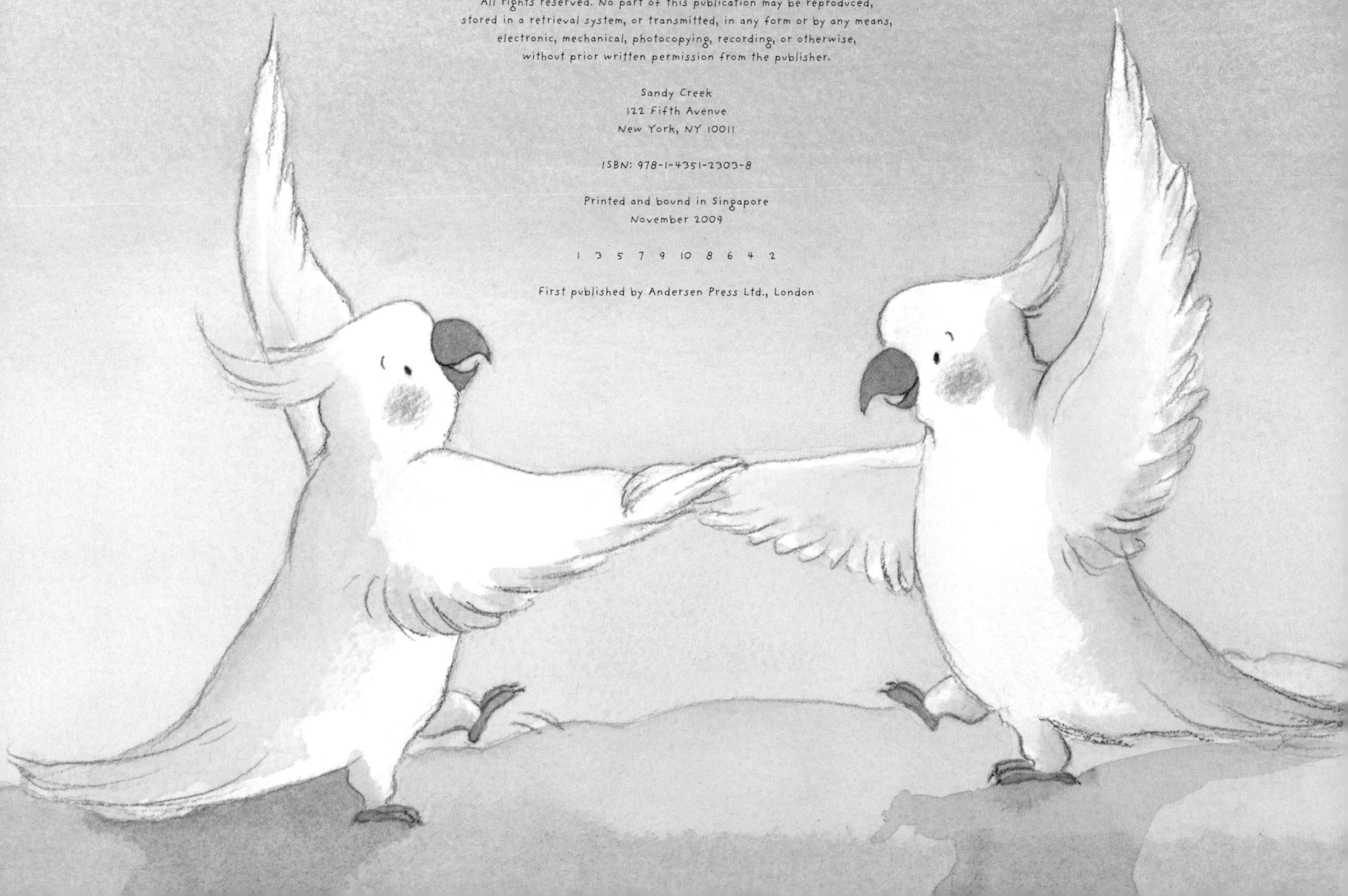

One, Two, Cockatoo!

Sarah Garson

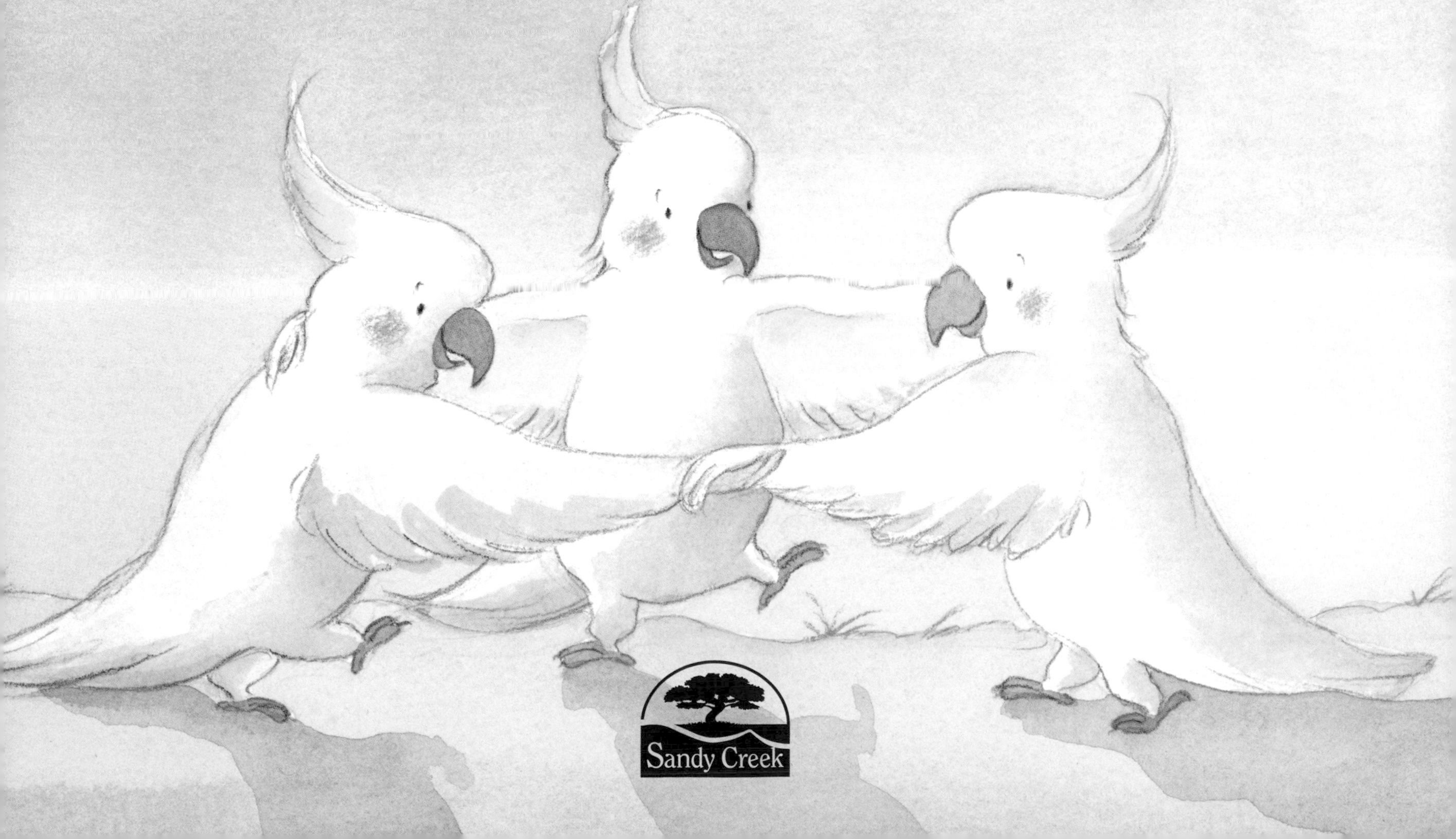

Sandy Creek

I One cockatoo on
his own in a tree.

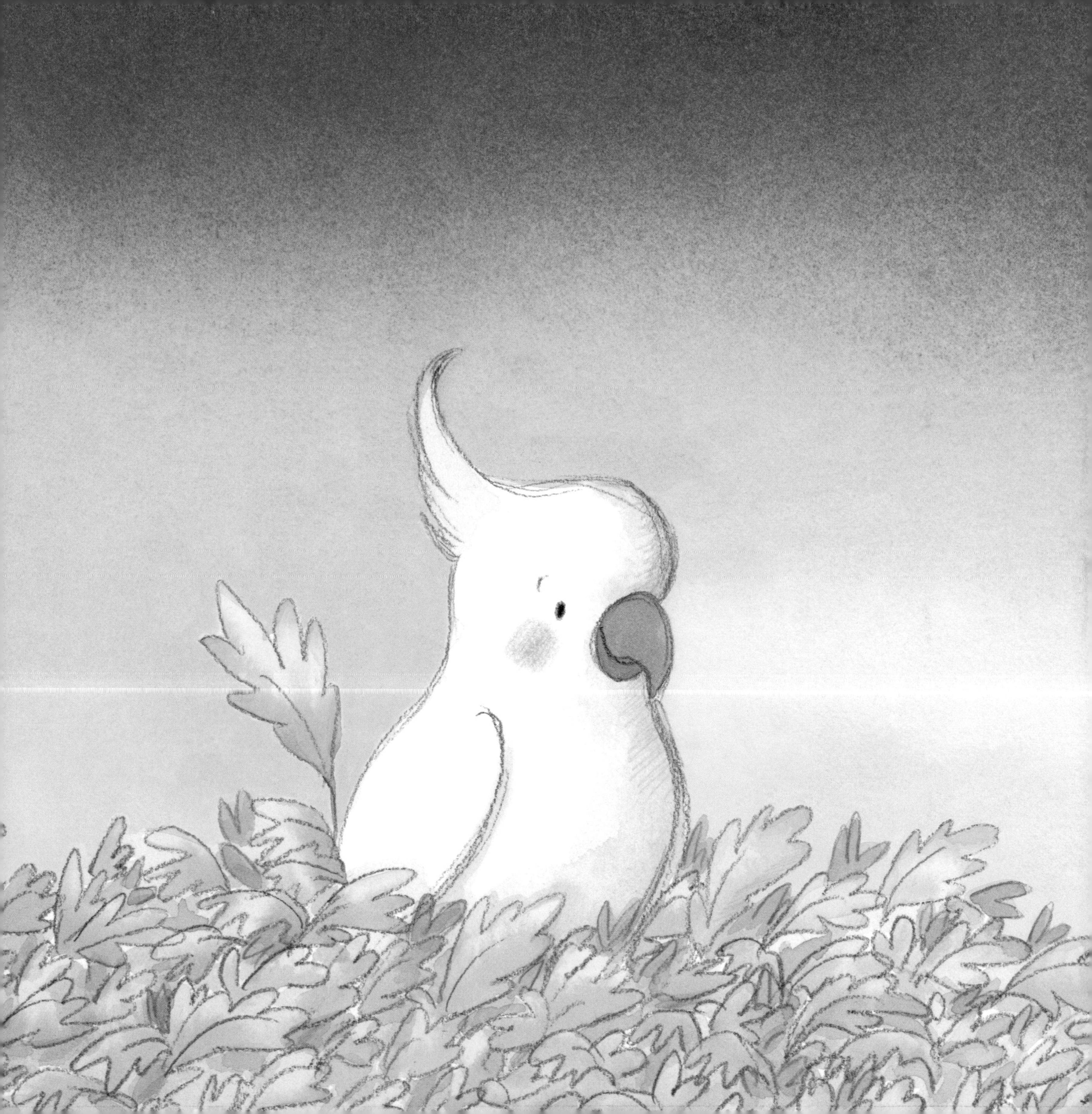

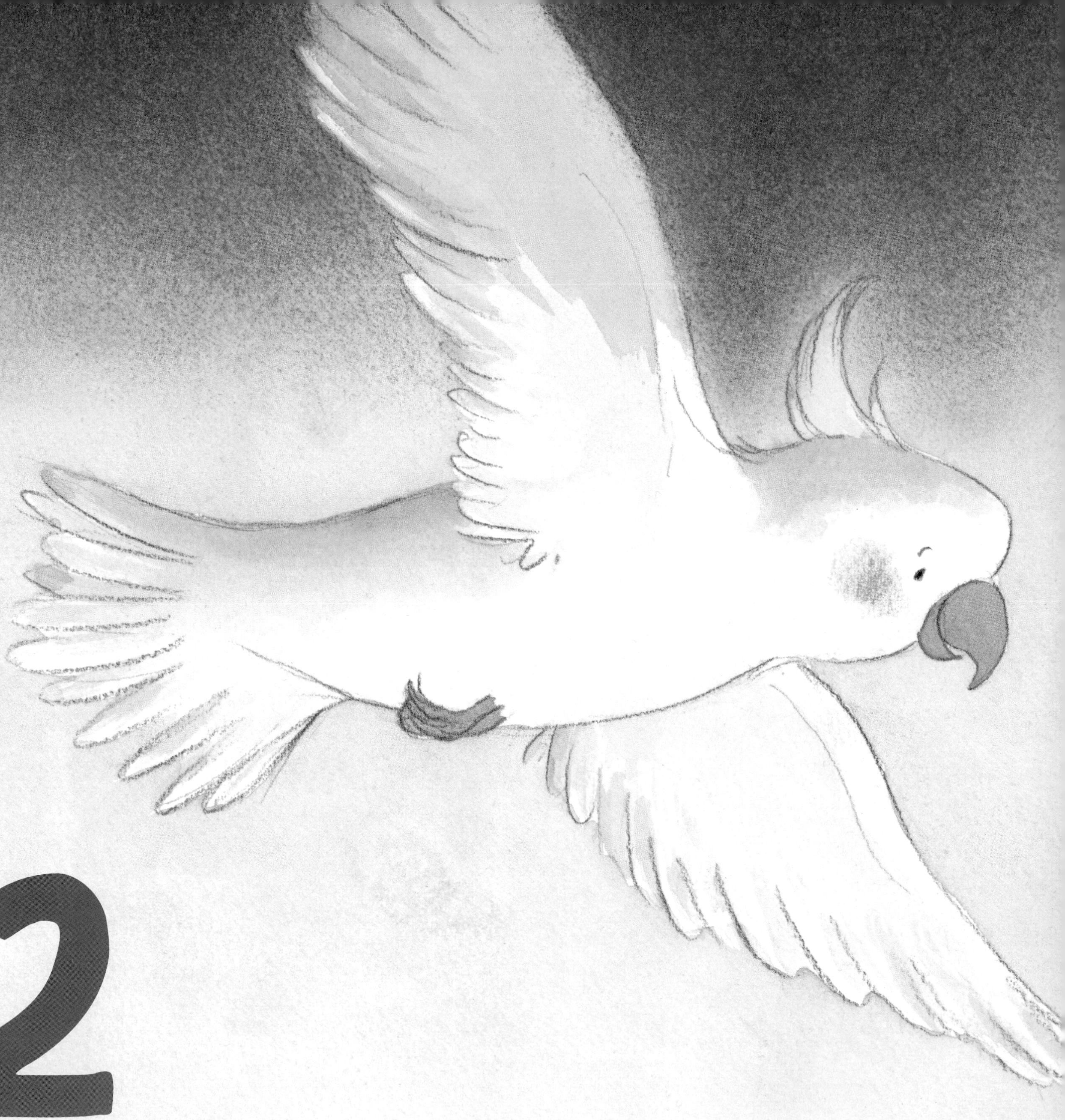

2

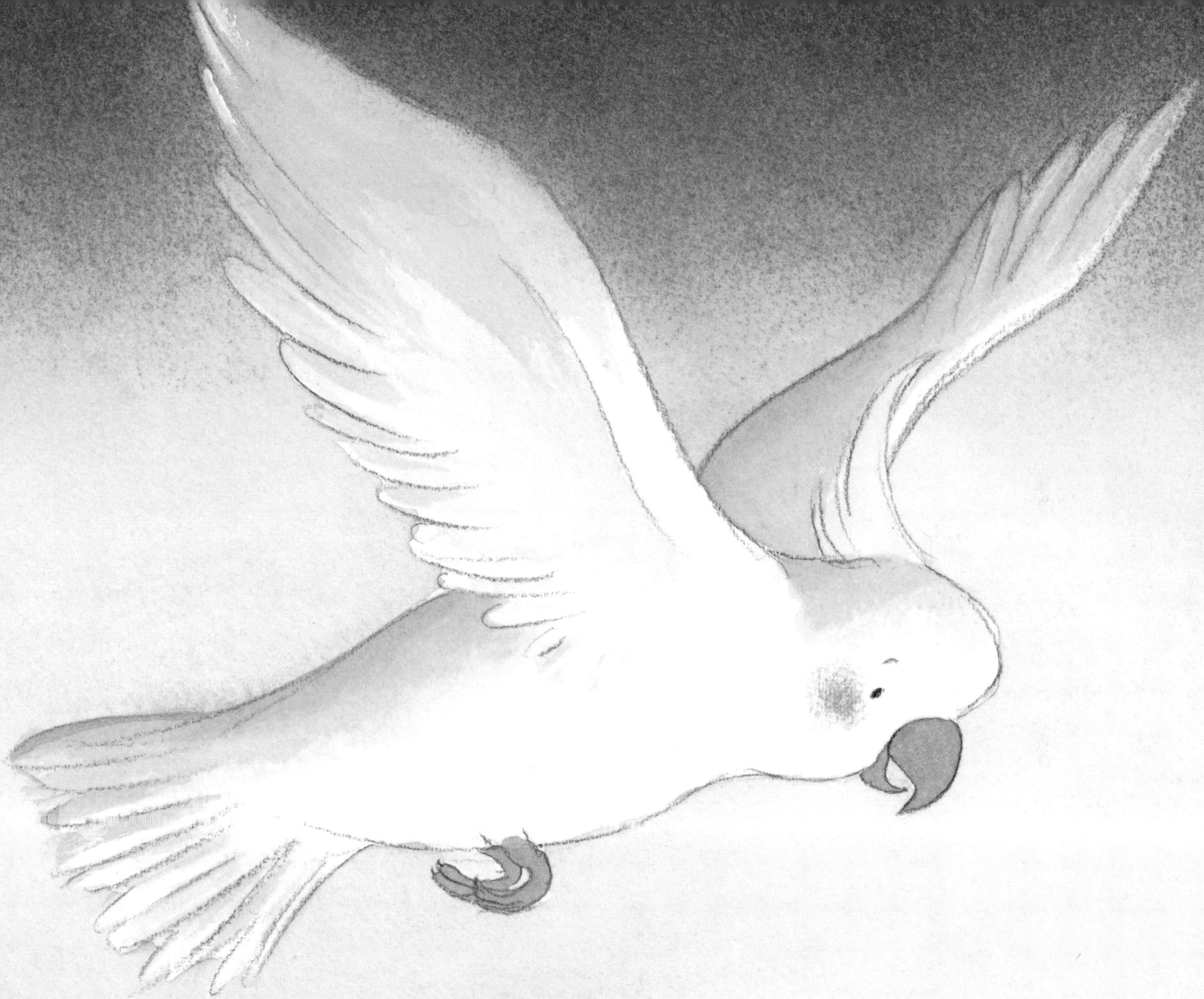

Two cockatoos fly over . . .

3

...that's three!

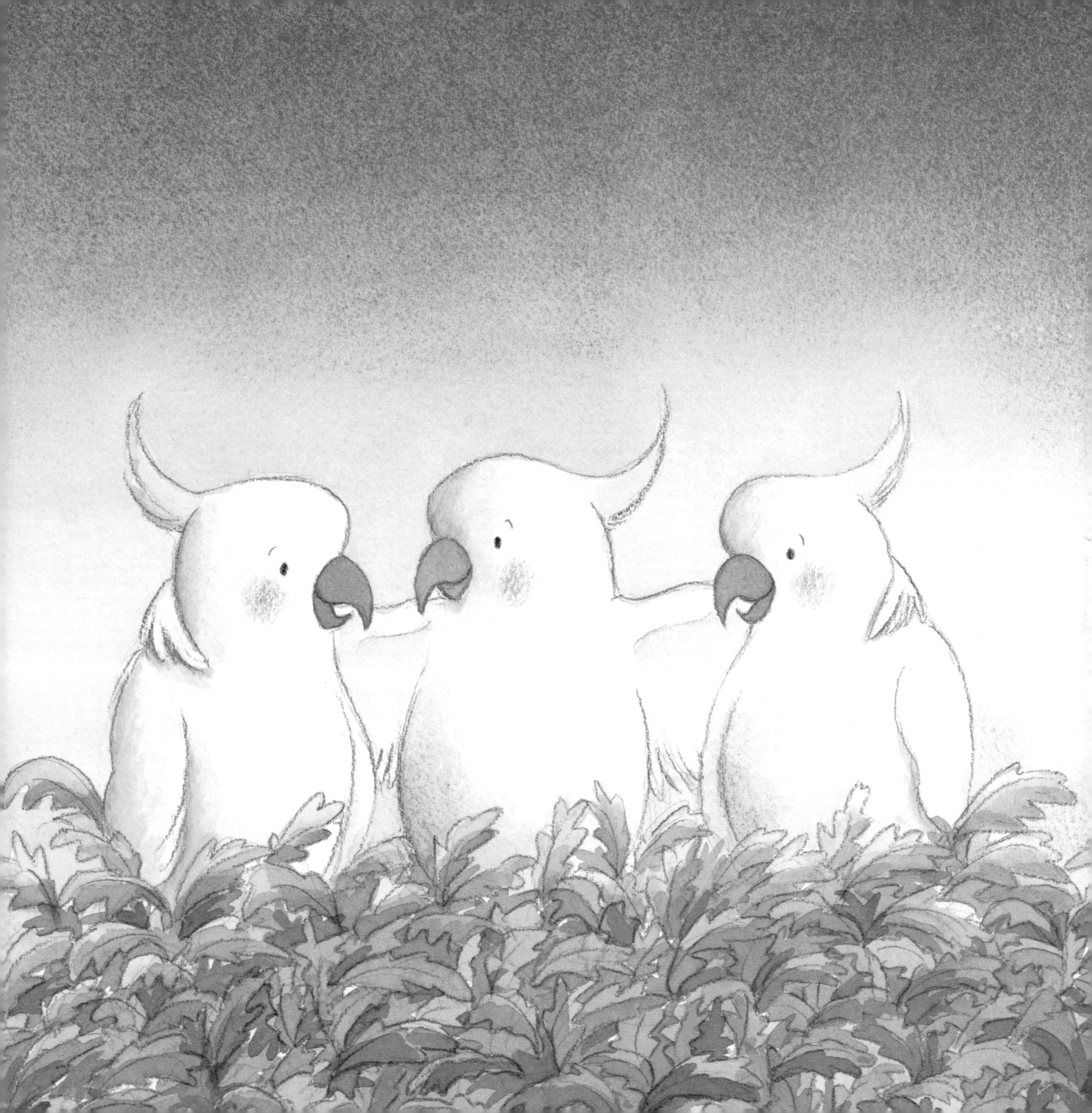

4 Four cockatoos
dancing a jive.

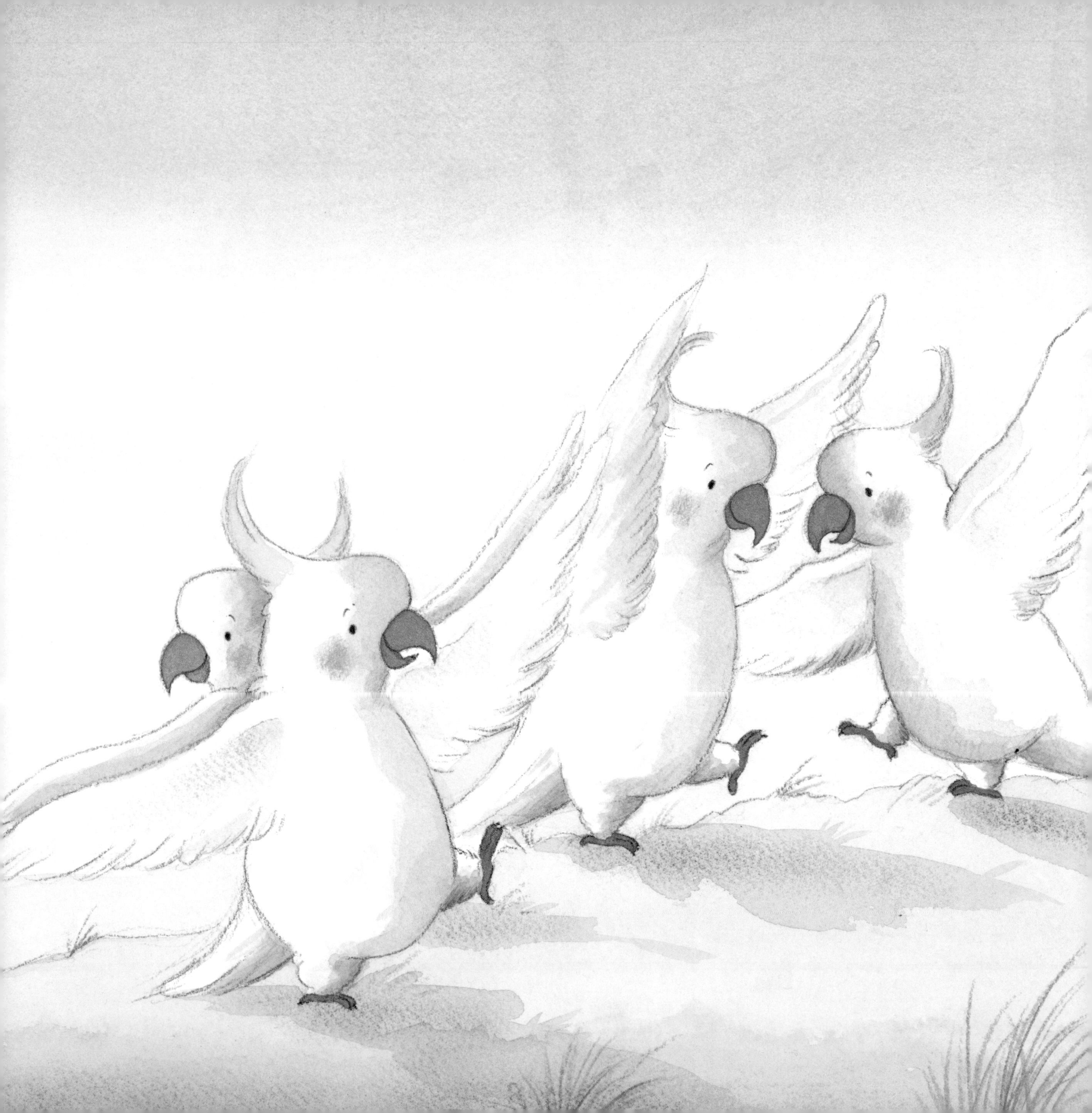

5

Another joins in and

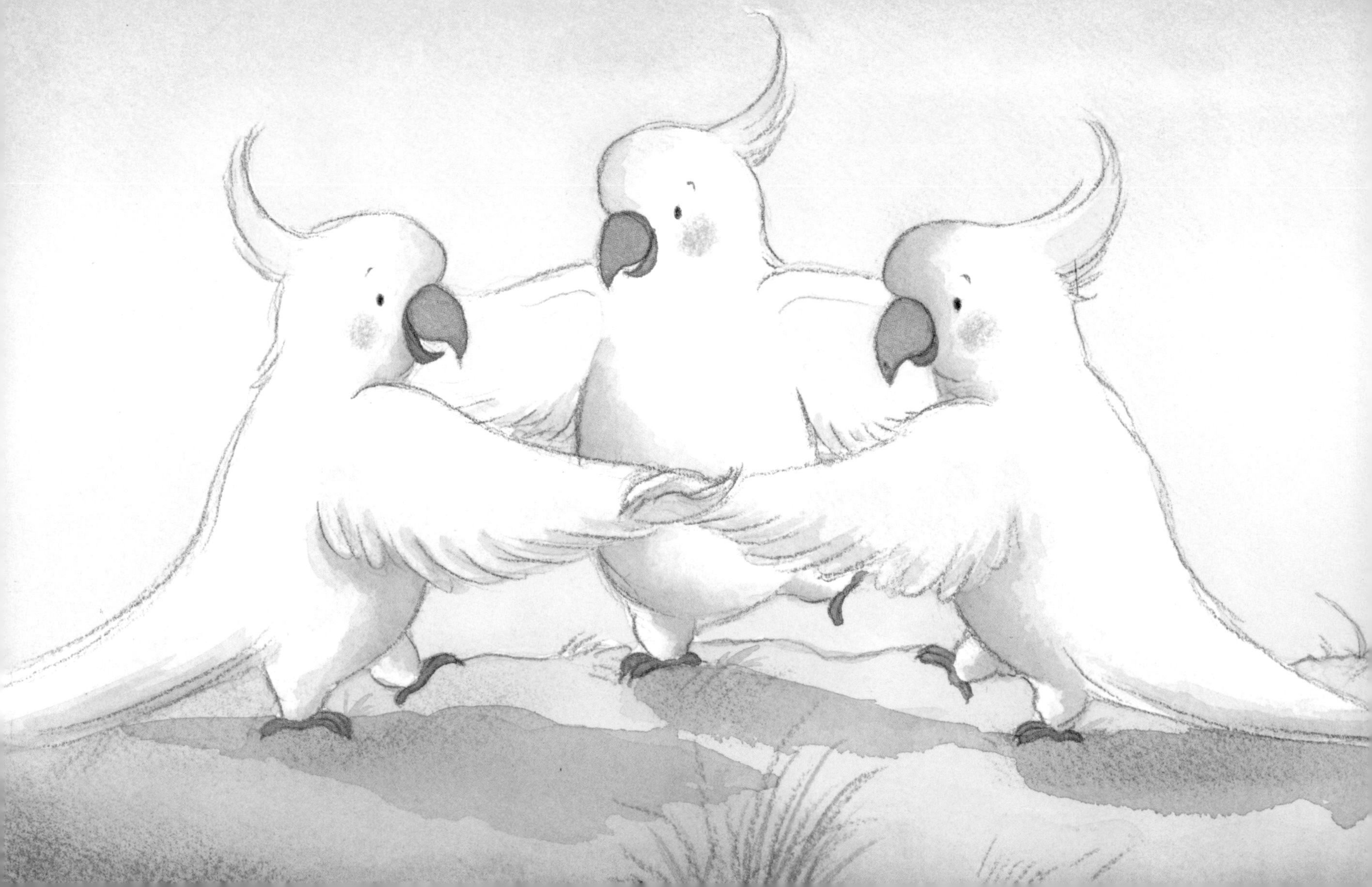

hey - presto — that's five!

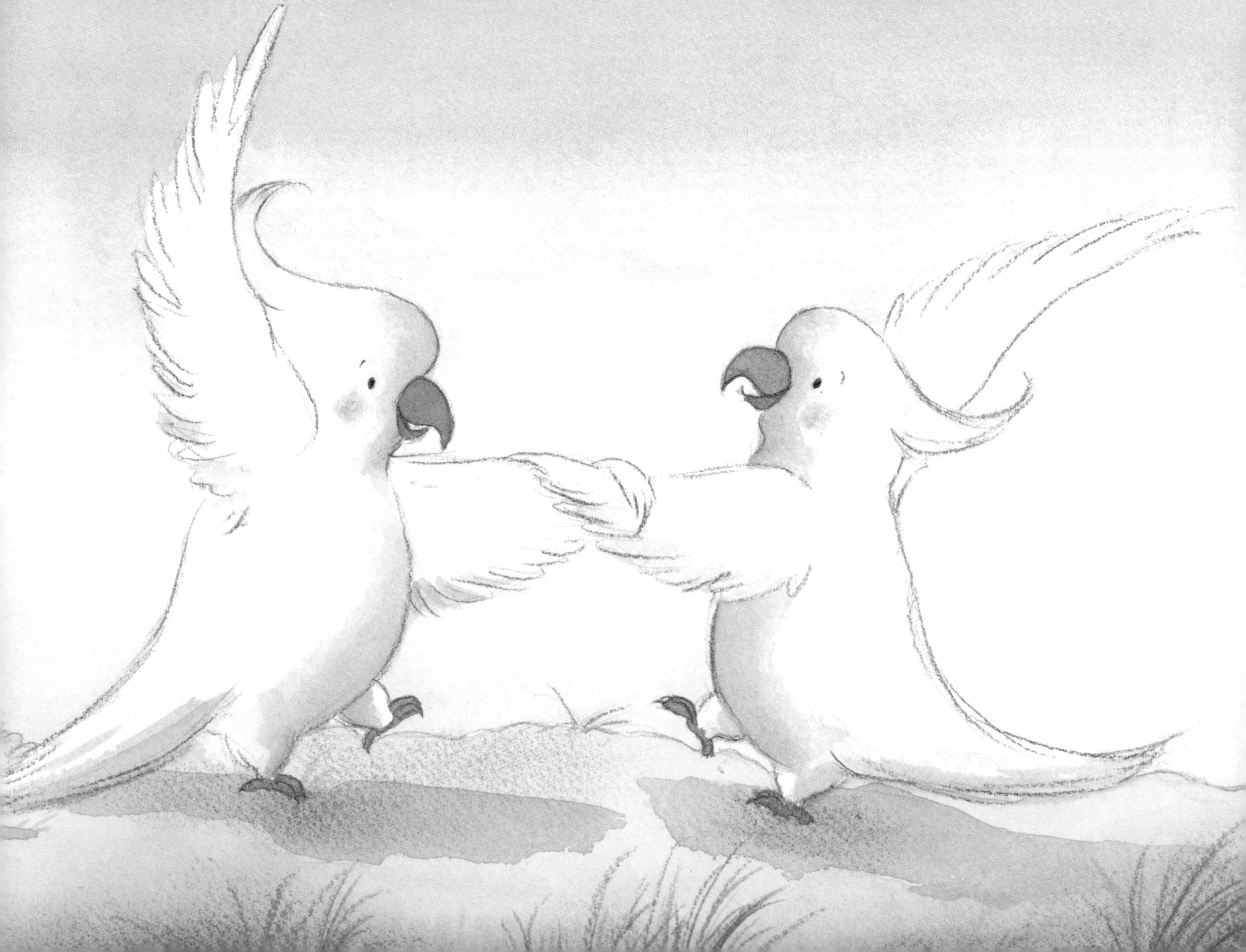

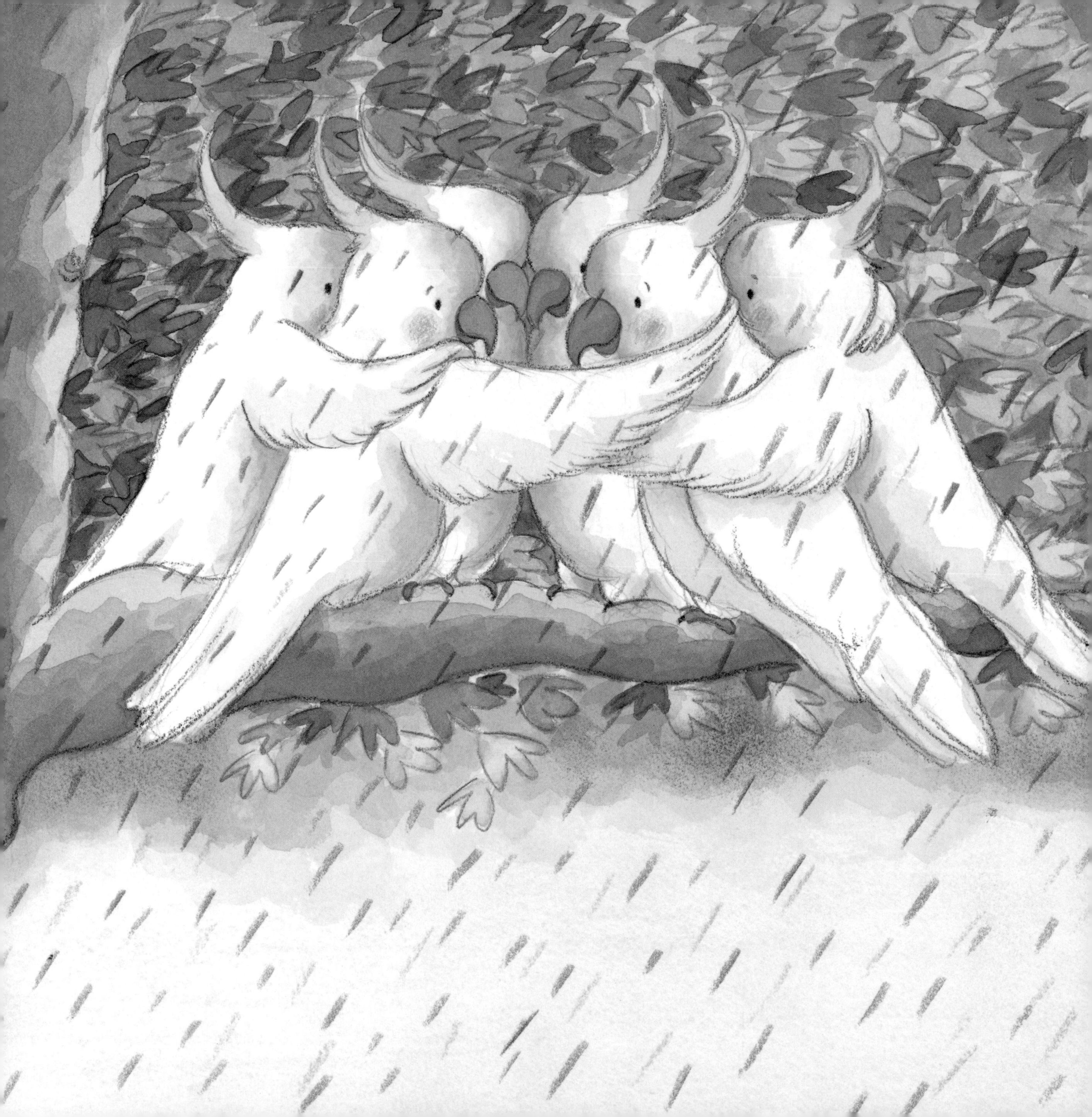

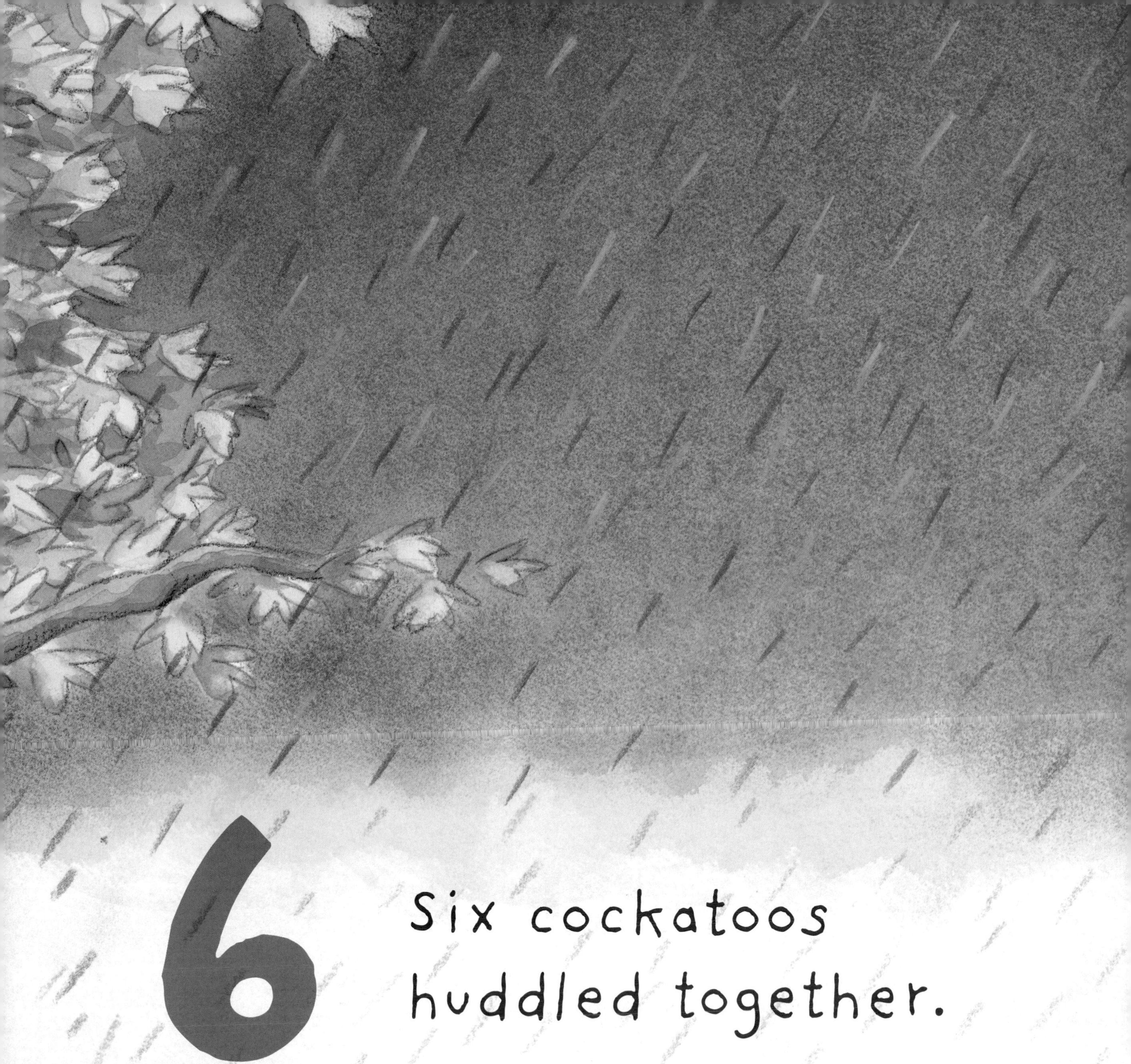

6

Six cockatoos huddled together.

7

Seven like splashing

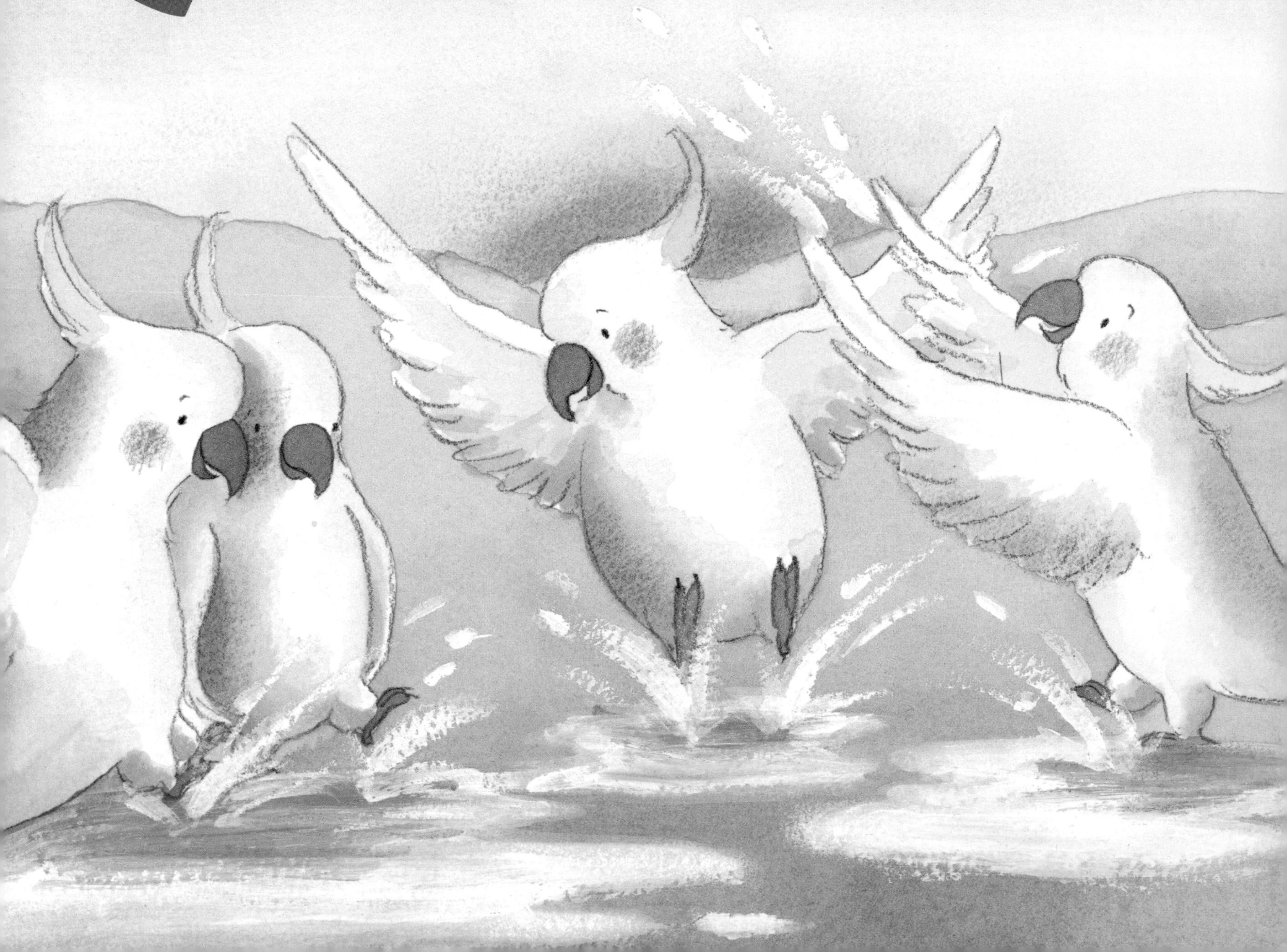

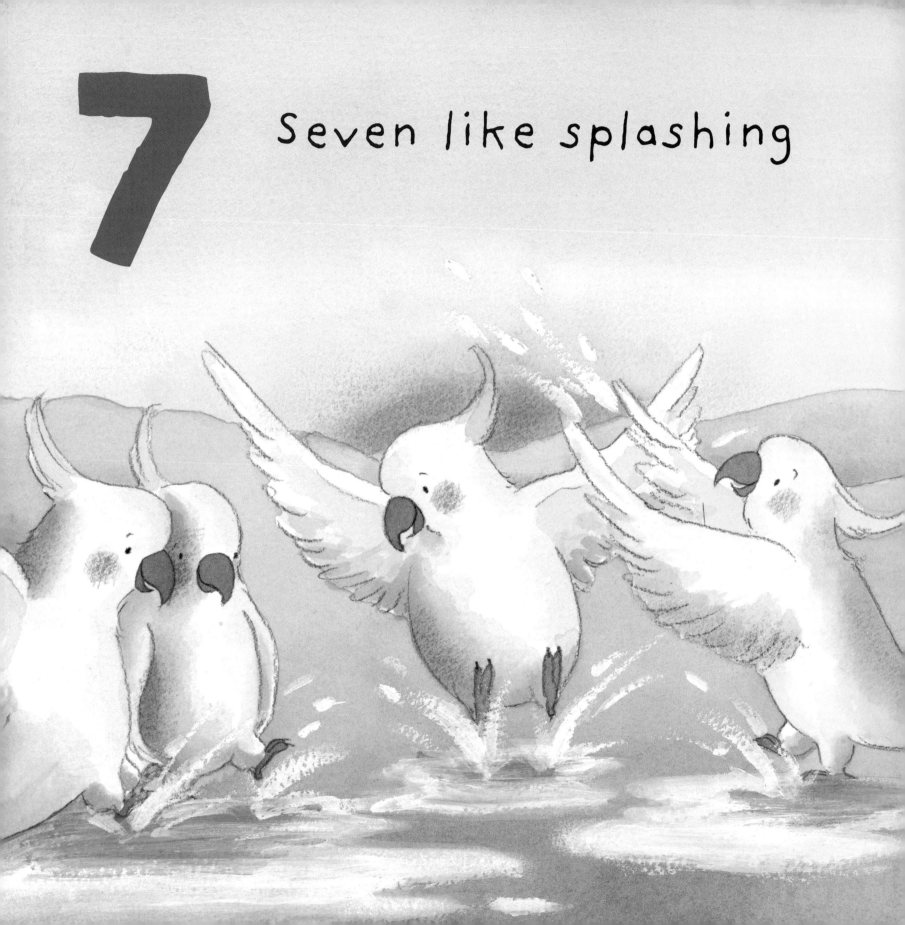

around in wet weather.

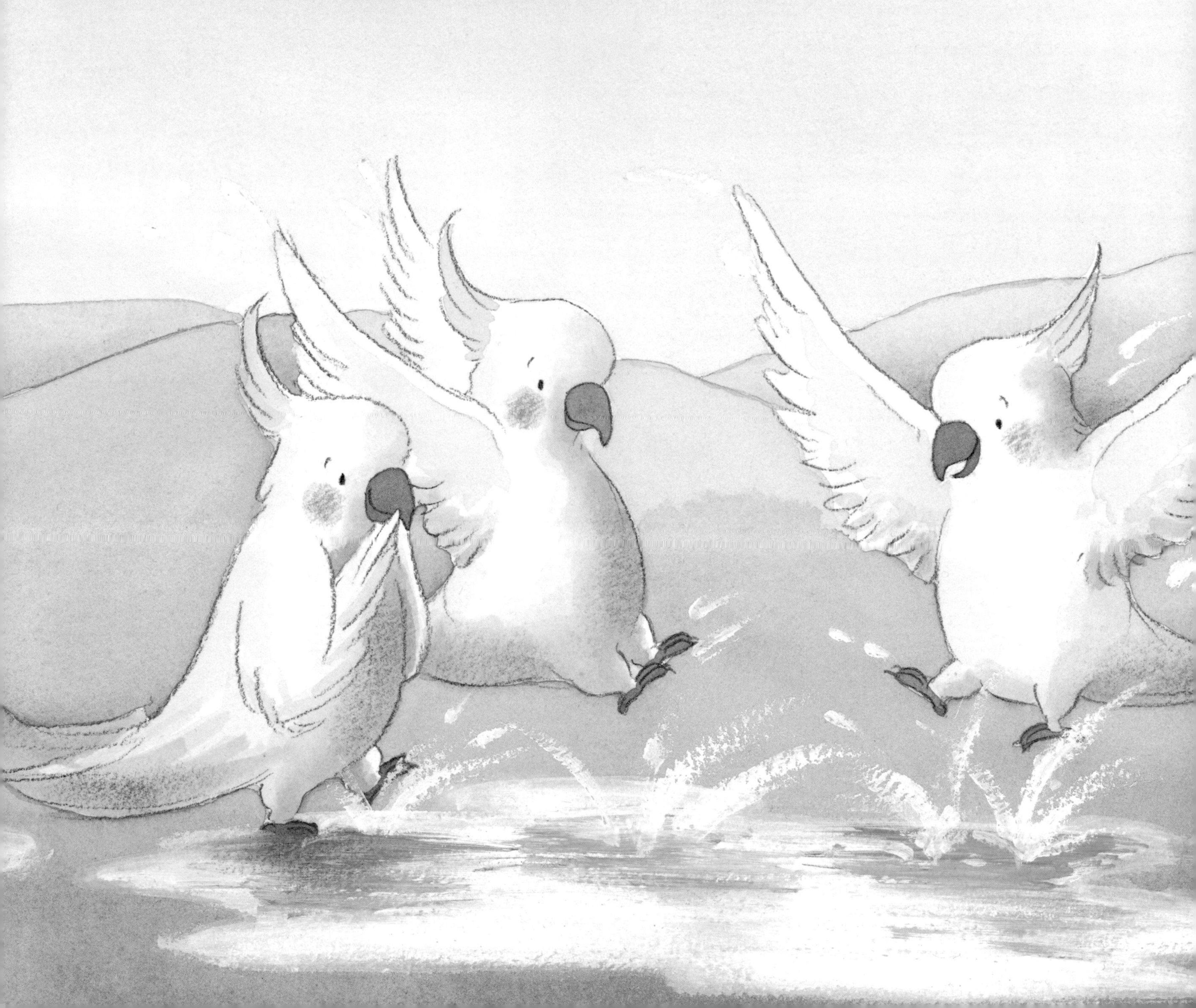

8

Eight cockatoos

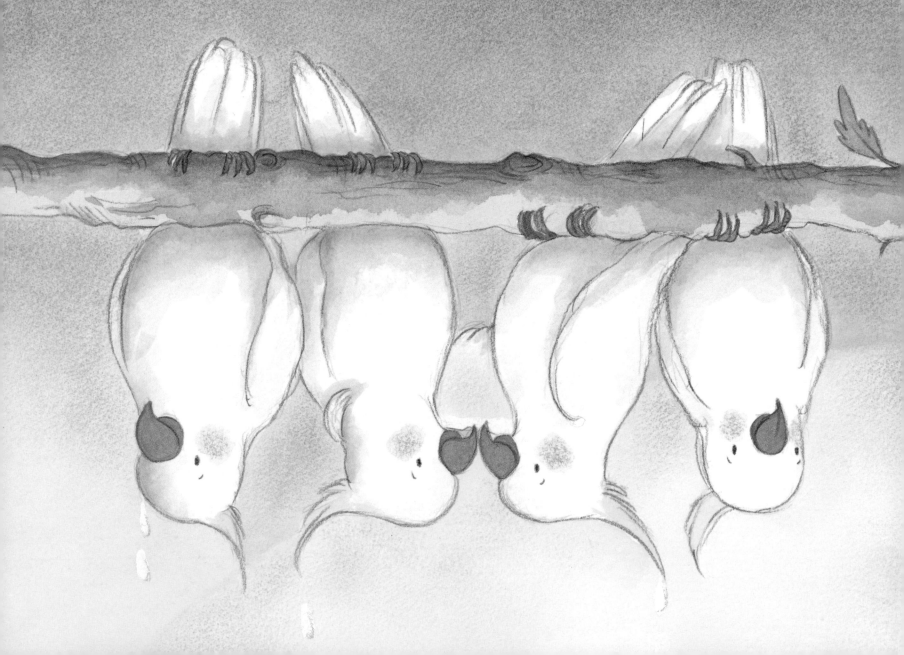

drying off in the sun.

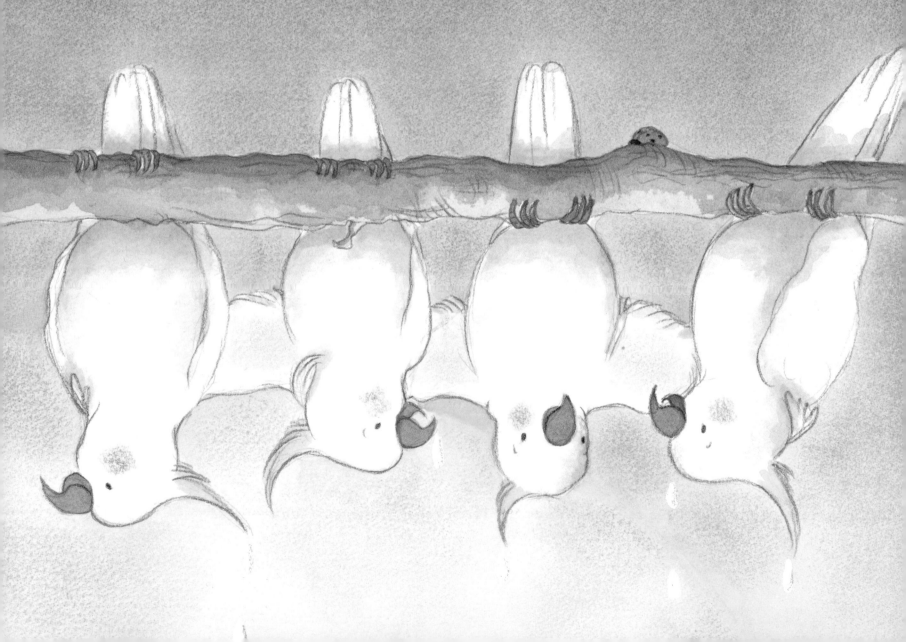

9

Nine cockatoos

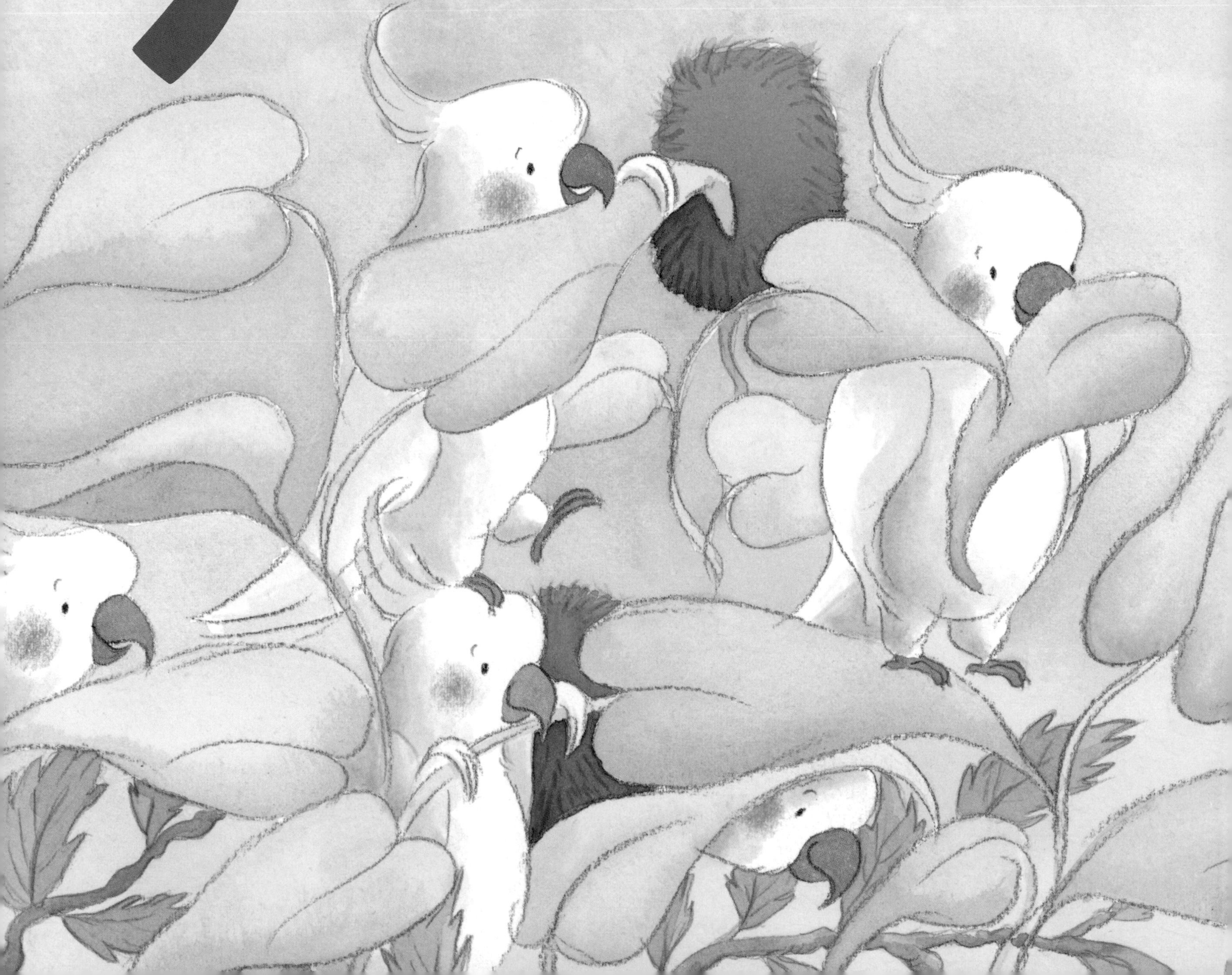

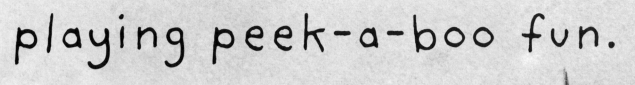

playing peek-a-boo fun.

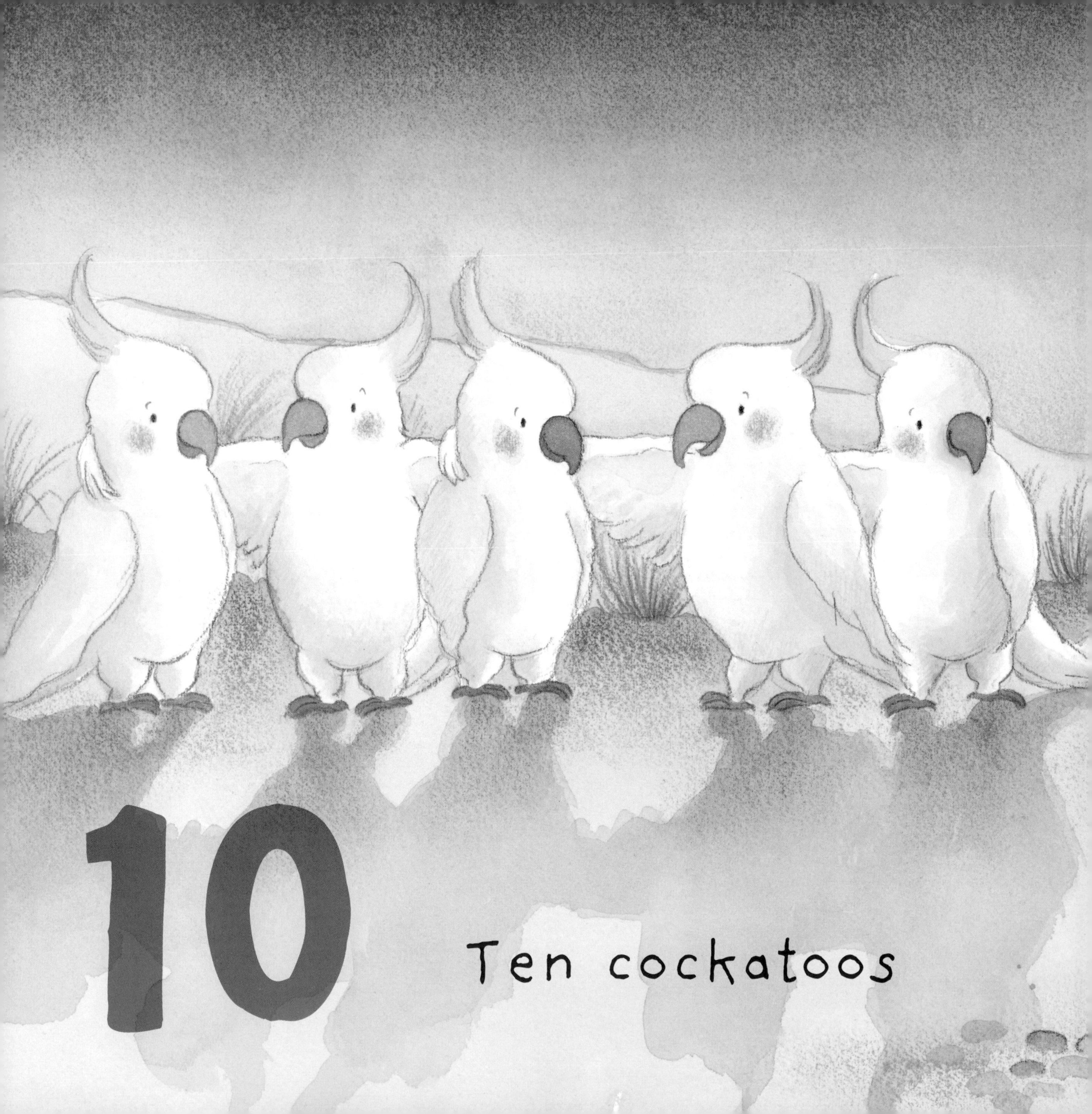

10

Ten cockatoos

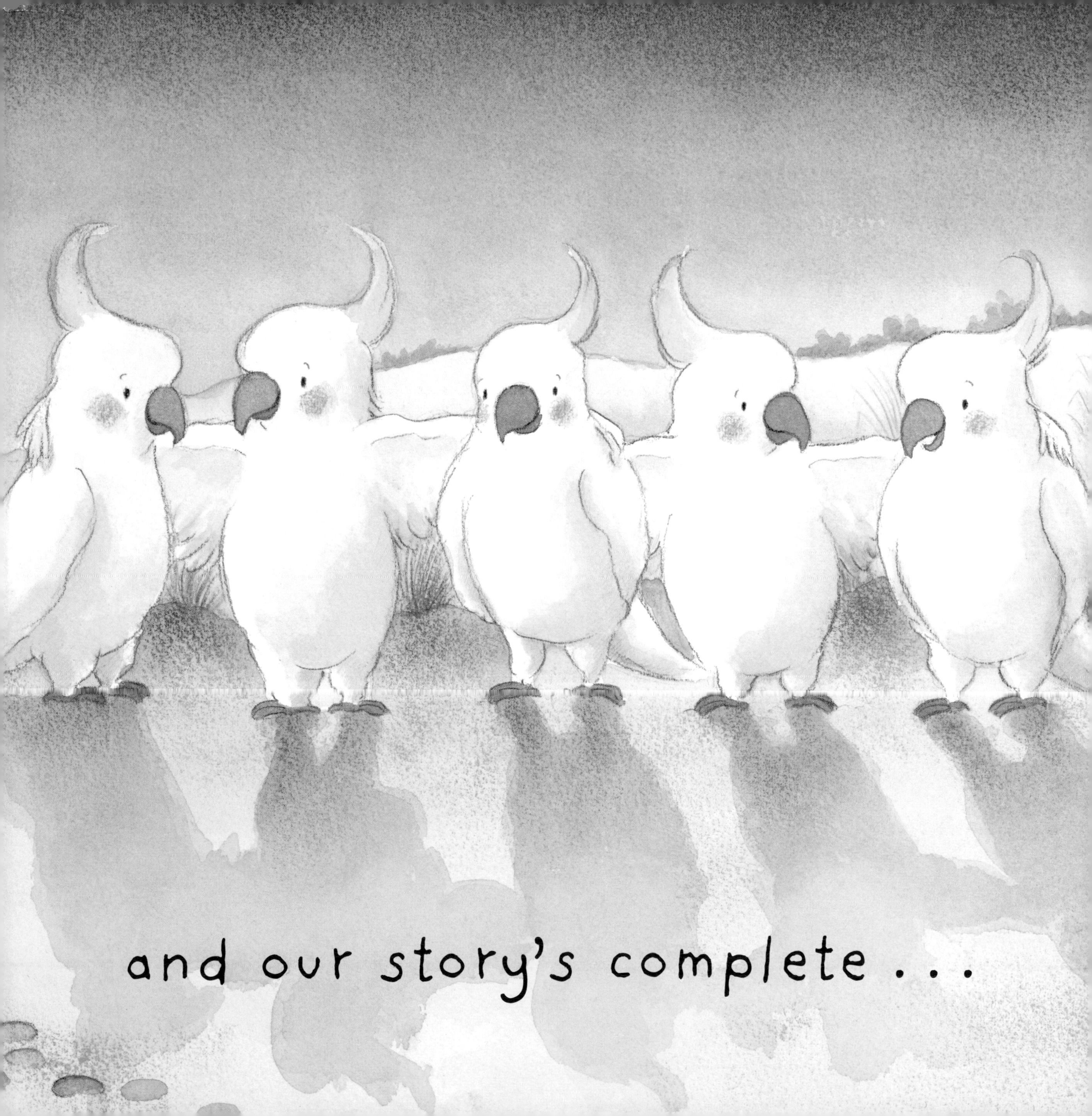

and our story's complete . . .

. . . but hold on

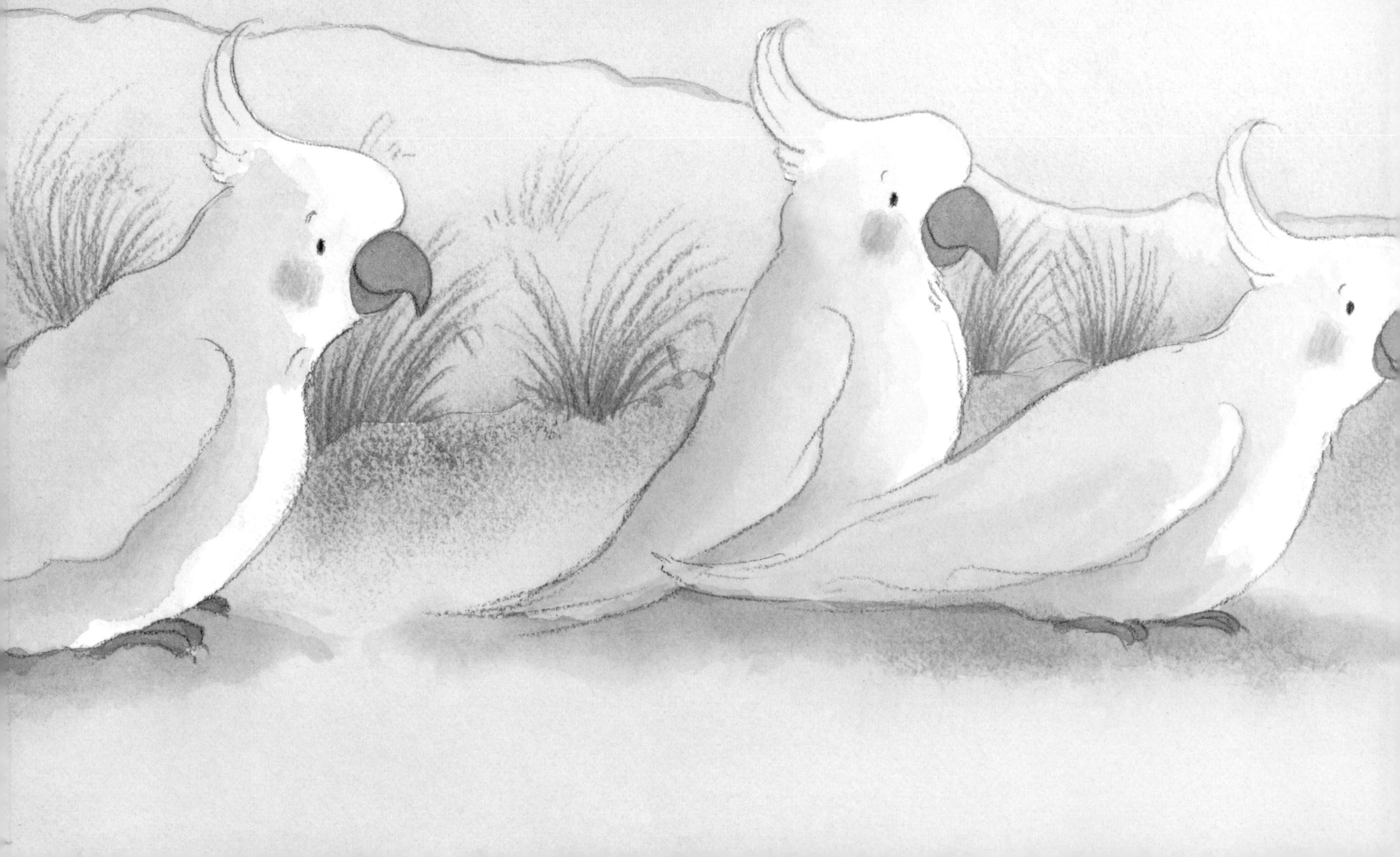

. . . what's that?

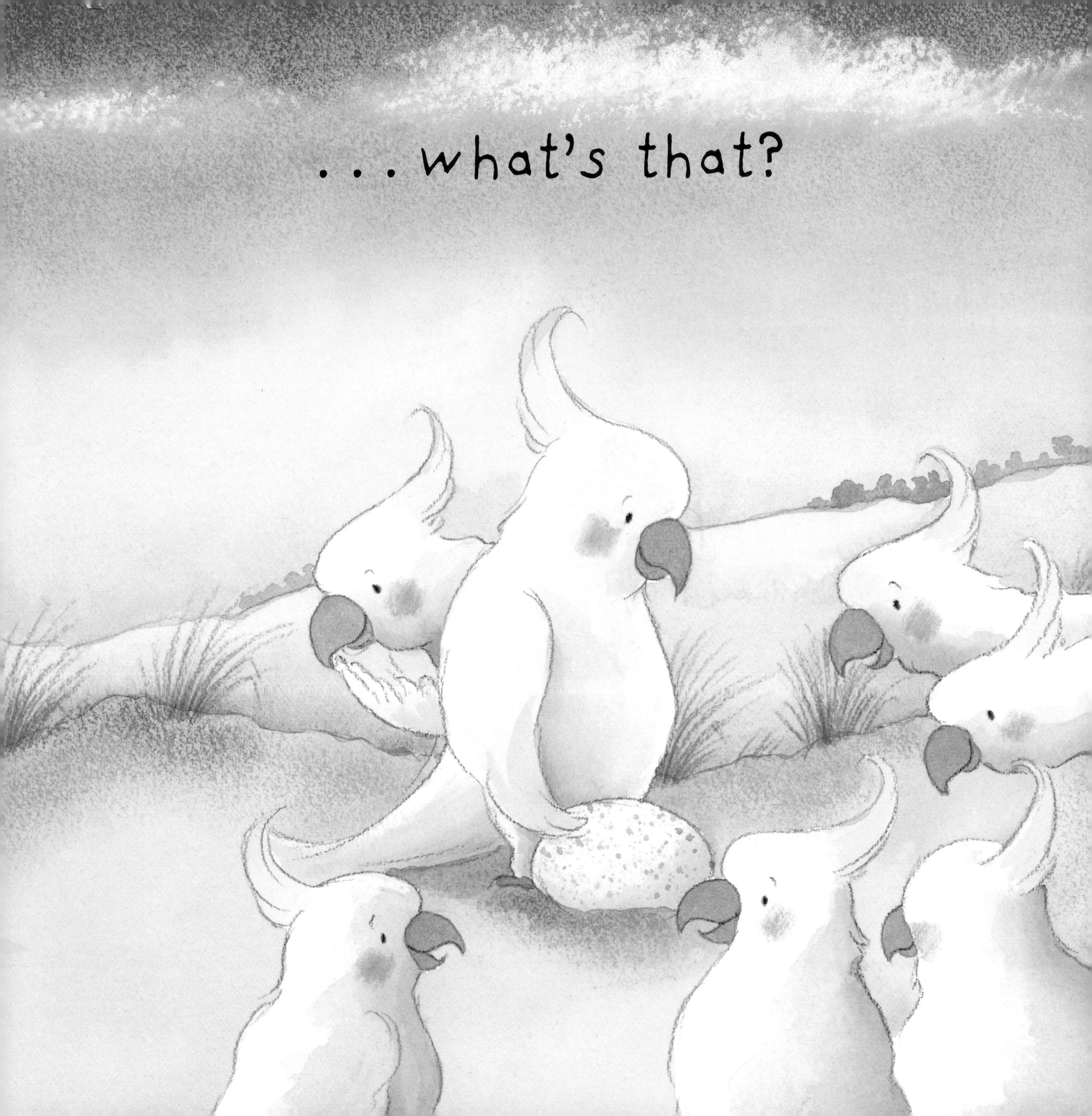

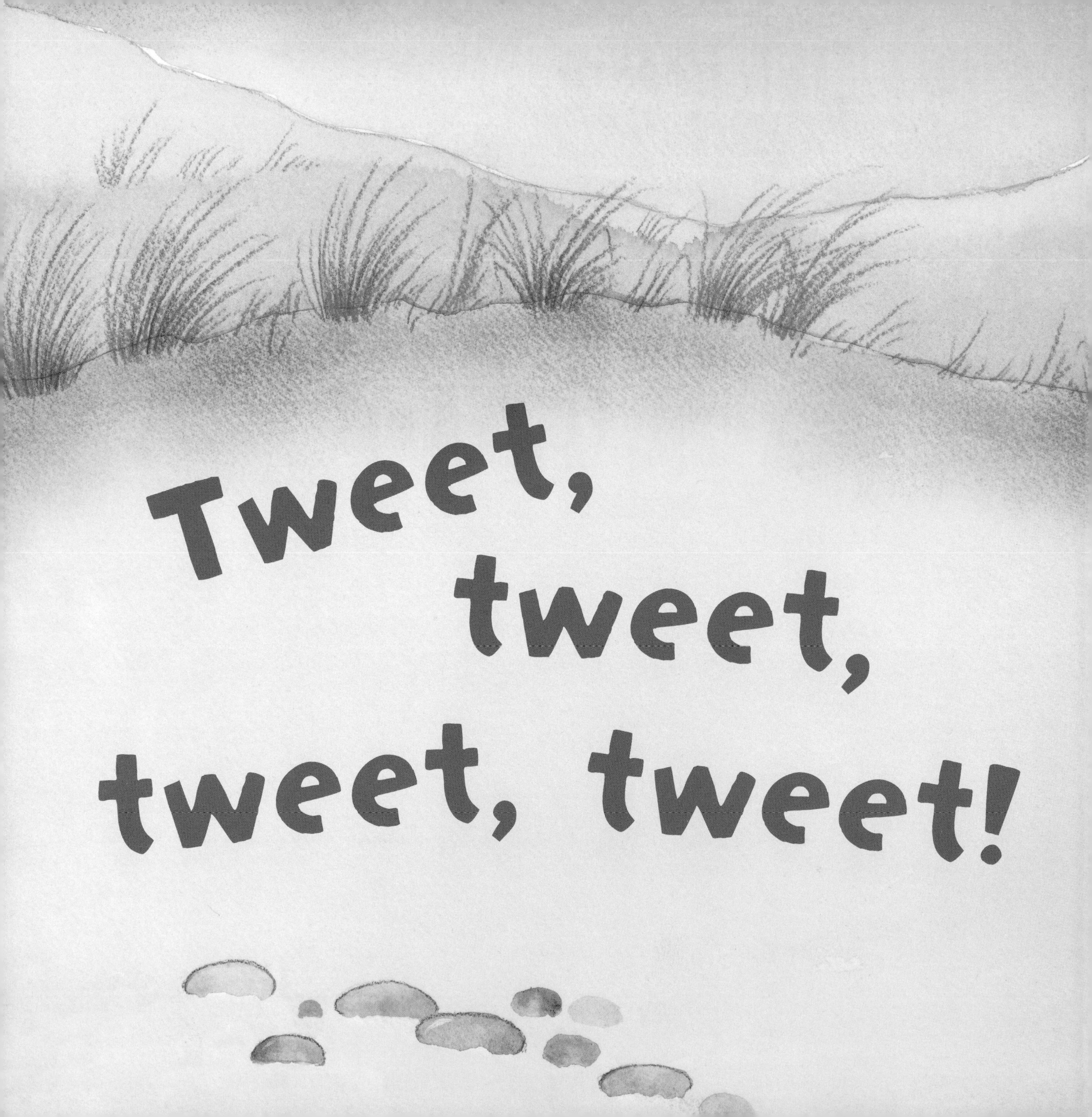

Tweet,
tweet,
tweet, tweet!

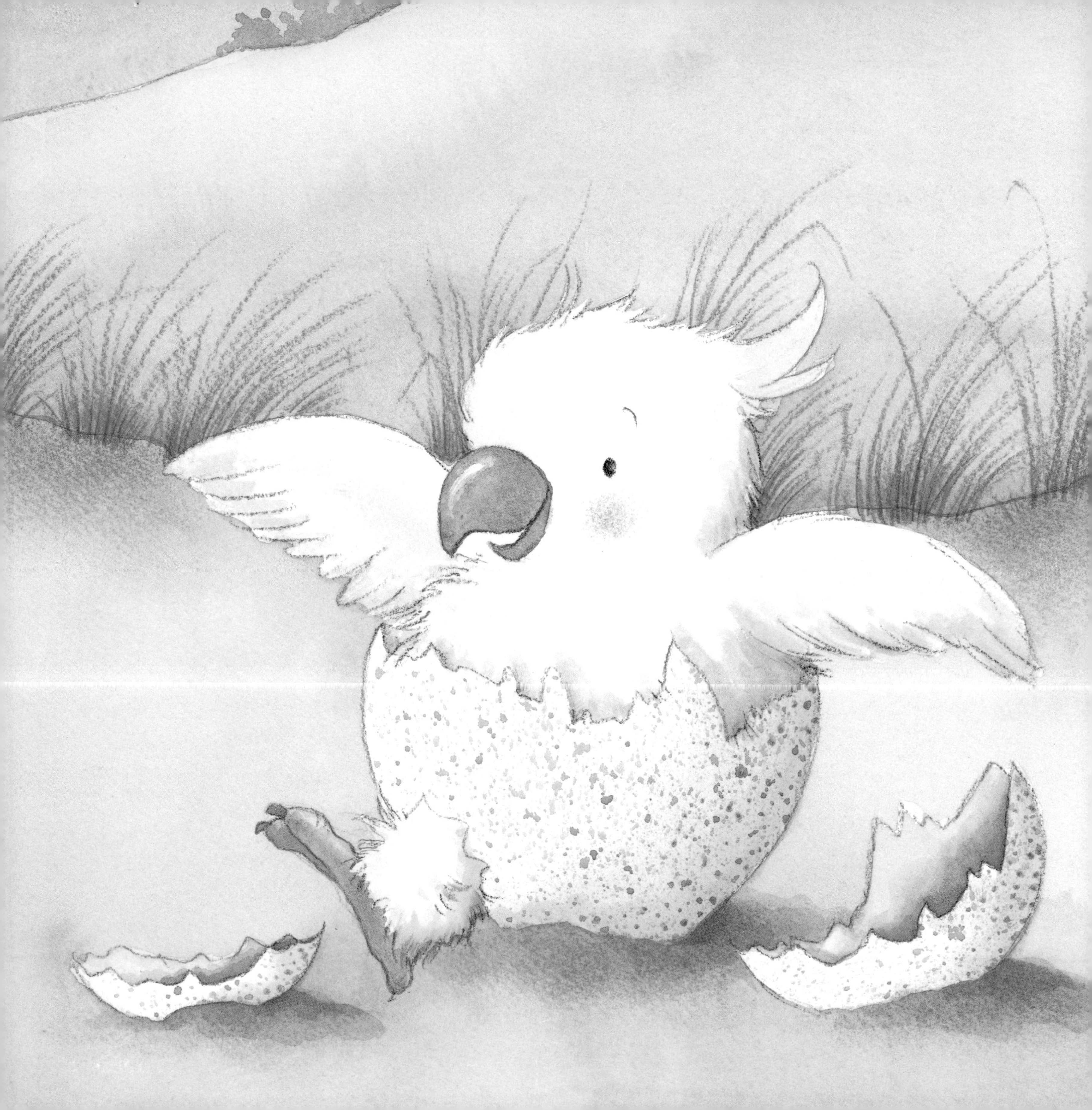

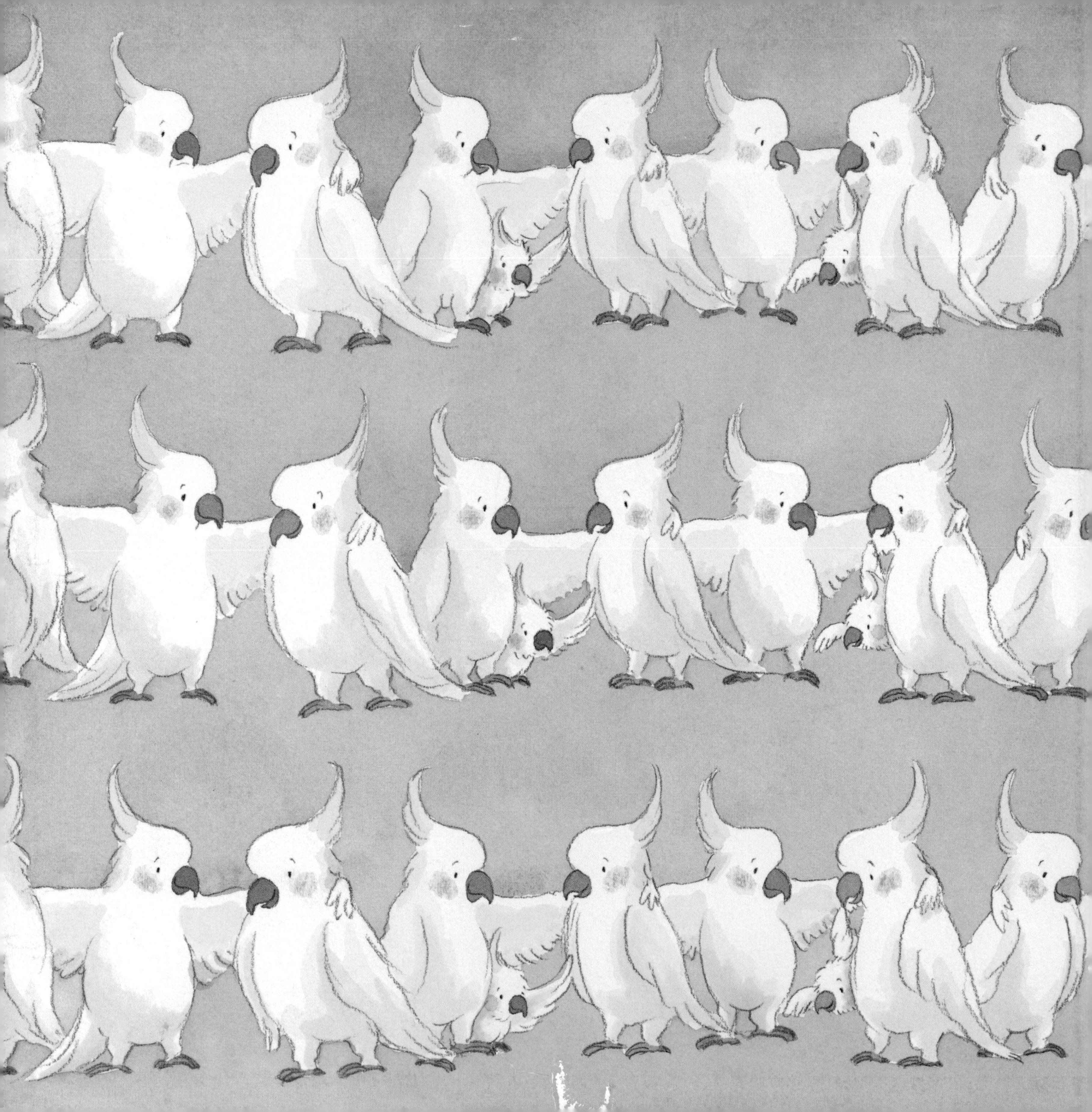